MASSACRE RANCH

The harsh outline of a star pinned inside his shirt and the pressure of two 'Wanted' posters folded inside his hat could prove to be Cliff Condon's passports to Boot Hill, as he entered rustler territory. As a lawman representing the cattlemen's association, he would receive a cold welcome, and as a bounty hunter, he would be fair game for thieves and murderers. But these were the chances Cliff had to take as he neared Massacre Ranch—a violent outfit heading for a make-or-break showdown and pulling down along with it Cliff and the two women who loved him.

MASSACRE RANCH

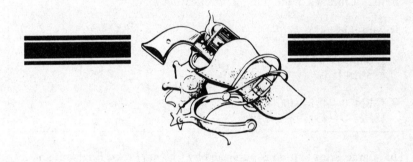

Orlando Rigoni

ATLANTIC LARGE PRINT
Chivers Press, Bath, England.
Curley Publishing, Inc.,
South Yarmouth, Mass., USA.

Library of Congress Cataloging in Publication Data

Rigoni, Orlando.
    Massacre Ranch / Orlando Rigoni.
        p.   cm.—(Atlantic large print)
    ISBN 1–55504–901–X (lg. print)
    1. Large type books.   I. Title.
[PS3568.I374M3 1989]
813′.54—dc19   89–30256
                                                                                      CIP

British Library Cataloguing in Publication Data

Rigoni, Orlando, *1917–*
    Massacre Ranch
    I. Title
    813′.54 [F]

    ISBN 0–7451–9500–8
    ISBN 0–7451–9512–1 Pbk

This Large Print edition is published by Chivers Press, England, and
Curley Publishing, Inc, U.S.A. 1989

Published by arrangement with Donald MacCampbell, Inc

U.K. Hardback ISBN 0 7451 9500 8
U.K. Softback ISBN 0 7451 9512 1
U.S.A. Softback ISBN 1 55504 901 X

Dedicated to my wife
Carolyn Belle
Whose nimble fingers do all the hard work.

MASSACRE RANCH

CHAPTER ONE

Cliff Condon halted his jaded horse at the edge of the churlish water and contemplated the wall on the opposite side. It was gouged, eroded, and painted by the brush of the gods in hues of vermilion, brown, and the darker red of dried blood. Looming against the blue of the clear desert sky, it was a forbidding challenge. The swift, terrible storm of the night before had left the rocks and ledges dripping, while small rivulets coursed down its wrinkled face, cutting the grooves deeper and loosening handfuls of gravel that rattled to its base.

Condon, removing his warped hat, brushed back his coarse, unruly hair, and the wrinkles in his forehead deepened as he scowled at the façade before him. Was this the end of the trail? The bone weariness of his lanky frame was a dull ache, and the hope and vengeance that had driven him all the way from Delgado, deep in Colorado, shriveled as he studied the three-hundred-foot cliffs that scoffed at him. There was no possible way for five hundred head of cattle to scale that wall. His eyes, under their heavy arched brows, found no semblance of a trail, not even a path. Holes resembling caves had been gouged into the breast of the cliff by the fury

1

of former floods, and they were still half full of the roaring, gory water that raced like a thousand devils down the rocky bed of the wash.

With a physical effort, he took his eyes off the wall, stared at the wild, painted flood, and shook his canteen. It was empty. Even this pigment-stained water would be better than the thirst that had hounded him the fifty miles from the Four Corners, that one place in the country where four states join. Clamping his hat on his head, he swung down from the saddle and led his horse to the edge of the turgid torrent. The long-limbed pinto plunged his muzzle into the water without concern for mud or color. Condon felt the stiffness of his knees, too long confined to stirrups, as he bent them to fill the canteen.

Two hundred miles of salt grass, mesquite, sand lizards and snakes, two hundred miles of heat and dust and dry, aching throat were ending here against a blank red wall. At first the tracks of the cattle had been easy to follow; nobody can spirit away five hundred head of cows without leaving a trace. The trail had been especially easy because this was the first time the rustlers had headed south toward the desolation of Tekabito and the Painted Desert. Mostly they drove their loot north to Denver or west toward Salt Lake City. Only a fool would dare the rough wilderness leading into nowhere.

Before he had reached the Hovenweep, Cliff Condon had begun to realize that there was a plan in the wild drive. Not only the fact that the cattle were driven south, but also the large number rustled, warned of a new band of thieves working the Delgado Range, and that they had left one man dead and another missing proved their caliber. There was a limit to the value of a cow, but there was no limit to the value of a man's life. The man who had been killed was his best friend, and the man who was missing was his brother, Arny. Headstrong and unbridled, Arny had fussed and feuded as younger brothers who resent authority will, but he was still his brother, and there is a peculiar tie that binds blood to blood which neither sin nor folly can sever.

The rustled herd had begun to split up before it reached the Four Corners country, bunches taking off in odd directions as though to confuse any pursuit. But Cliff read a pattern in the tracks, and felt sure the various bunches would rendezvous at some appointed place before they reached their destination. After following several branching trails, he had decided that the rendezvous would be south of the Colorado River, near the Arroyo Diablo. Then the storm had struck yesterday when he was near his destination. He had taken refuge under an overhanging cutbank, lucky that the whole

3

ledge had not crumbled upon him under the lashing rain. Now here he was in the Arroyo Diablo, with all the tracks completely scoured from the earth.

Sitting on his haunches, his mud-caked chaps straining across his knees, he studied the face of the cliff. There was the faint outline of a trail that had been beaten by the cloudburst, but at best it was the trail of wild animals wandering down from the breast of the Mesa in search of water. He pursed his lips, and his deep brown eyes searched the cliff with practiced care. Yes, there *was* a trail. He doubted a horse could manage it, but if any horse could, his paint horse, Bolo, named because he had the speed of a bullet, could scale it.

Cliff Condon looked at the sky. It was getting late, the sun having already vanished beyond the rim of the mesa, cloaking the Arroyo Diablo in a shroud of velvet. He felt the walls on either side of him like giant pincers, for the Arroyo Diablo was no mere arroyo; it was a deep gulch gouged into the earth through a million years of erosion. He had no desire to spend a night in the dismal spot and, mounting his horse, he forded the still healthy current and reached a narrow bank on the opposite side.

Dismounting, he looped his arm through the reins and started to climb the dim trail on foot, his horse following. What could have

4

been a wide, foot-sure trail, the deluge had whittled to a mere toehold. He inched his way up, Bolo following with scrambling hooves, until the toehold widened and the going became easier. Reaching a point where a small ravine cut back into the face of the cliff, the trail turned and followed the ravine up toward the summit. Here Cliff stopped to get his wind and to give the horse a breather. Twilight was deepening, and he had no desire to be caught on the face of the cliff in the dark. He felt the harsh outlines of the star badge pinned inside his shirt, and the pressure of the wanted posters which were folded inside the sweat band of his hat. A rep for a cattlemen's association found a cold welcome in rustler territory, and a bounty hunter was fair game for thieves and killers.

He had sought neither job, but they had been thrust upon him. The cattlemen on the Delgado range would not stand for any large scale rustling, and the murder of Hal Chester, his long-time friend, had made him a prime candidate for the job. He had no intention of parading his purpose or his identity until he was sure of his ground.

Trudging forward, he found the trail flattening out toward the top; so, mounting the big pinto, he proceeded to ride the rest of the distance. It was almost dark by now. The thickening brush along the trail took strange shapes; the smell of piñon and juniper lent

5

their acrid scent to the fresh wind sweeping across the top of the mesa. As he came out onto flatter ground, the squat trees closed in about him, their gnarled limbs like arms raised in supplication.

No longer able to see the trail clearly, Cliff Condon gave his horse his head, trusting to his sharper vision to find a path through the thickening grove of trees and rabbit brush. Suddenly Bolo threw up his head and snorted. Like a disembodied thing, a voice came from some distance away in the thicket of trees.

'You've passed the boundary sign, hombre! We don't cotton to trespassers!'

The smash of the bullet struck Condon before the fury of the sound, and his right side went numb from the shock. He felt himself slipping from the saddle and tried desperately to grab the pommel, but his right hand was useless. Throwing himself to the left side of his horse, he hooked his right spur into the saddle girth in an effort to anchor himself. At the same time he urged the big horse into a wild run through the brush and trees. He felt the branches clawing at him like bony fingers, but he hung on.

If there was pursuit, he could not hear it. Warm blood flooded down his side, and the pain of his body became a living thing. Then the pain seemed to lessen, and the red haze thickened. The spur broke loose from the saddle girth, and he felt himself slipping—slipping—slipping into oblivion . . .

★   ★   ★

Condon stirred and opened his eyes. The light was dim, but whether it was dawn or dusk he didn't know. How many hours had he lain there? This must be a dream. But the dead did not dream. The excruciating pain in his side was no dream, either. He closed his eyes against the lash of fever, and felt water trickling down his throat. This was another dream to harry and goad him. He even dreamed of soft fingers bathing his brow. Then the fever overwhelmed him once more, blotting out the dream and the pain.

Twice more he had the same sense of painful consciousness, but the third time the light was stronger, the fever in his blood a warm caress. His side had become a dull throb, and he was amazed to find his right arm bound against his side with clean bandages. His chaps had been removed and were lying beside him, with his gun belt. His gun was near his left hand, and his hat was propped over his eyes, shading them. Turning his head with difficulty, he saw a canteen near his left hand, the top unscrewed. He reached for it and, removing the cap with his teeth, let the cool water run down his throat. He realized somebody had been giving him water before, for his thirst was not great. Near the canteen stood a covered bowl, with the handle of a spoon protruding.

Reaching carefully for the bowl lest he spill its contents, he drew it toward him, and as his hand removed the lid he heard a low growl near his feet. He had heard wolves many times, but he could not imagine a wolf lying there waiting for his survival. Painfully he tried to raise his head, and realized it was supported by a pad of some sort. Someone must have worked very fast to have accomplished all this in one night—bandages, water, food, comfort. He heard the growl again, and forced his head up as far as he could. At his feet lay the saggy body of a dog, a dog that looked like a wolf, apparently left there by someone to guard him, or to keep him from escaping.

'Hello, boy,' Condon tried to say, but it came out garbled and vague. He realized then how he was struggling for breath. Even the effort of raising his head and speaking to the dog proved almost too much for him. He lay for a while in a half-stupor. When he could breath evenly again, he removed the cover from the bowl, which contained a rich, thick soup. Turning his head to the side, he was able to spoon the soup into his mouth without spilling too much of it.

Again exhausted by the effort, he lay back,

a whimper of pain escaping as the action strained his wound. The big dog, more wolf-like when he stood erect, walked to his side and, after licking the hand that protruded from the bandages, lay down close to Condon's wounded side. Even though the lukewarm soup had revived him, it provided but a small amount of the energy needed to combat the feverish weakness that devoured him. Once more he fell into a deep stupor.

The next time he awoke to the touch of soft hands bathing his face with cool water. He felt the dampness of his forehead where the coarse hair had been brushed back. It was dark, but he knew instinctively that he was being tended by a woman, for no man could be so gentle yet thorough. At first he was afraid to speak lest this prove to be another dream and the shadowy figure bending over him an imagined angel.

'Who are you?' he asked, amazed at how much stronger his voice was.

'That's not important,' the girl responded in a strange, quiet voice that held sorrow and rebellion. 'The name is Naomi.'

'To me it's important. You saved my life.'

'I would have saved the life of a wounded coyote.'

'You sound bitter,' Cliff said, wishing he could see her face.

'I am bitter—bitter against killing, bitter against stealing, cheating, bitter against sin.'

'If you hadn't found me last night, I would be dead,' Cliff said flatly.

'Last night? It was not so easy as that,' she said gently.

With his left hand he felt of his shirt and found the star badge still pinned inside, and noticed his hat at his side.

'Where did you find my hat?' he asked.

'Back on the trail your horse made,' she said, finished with the bathing. 'But it was not last night I found you; it was three nights ago. This is the fourth night. I prayed for you every night, I smuggled things here to keep you alive. I have slept very little during that time, and I did not do all this to have you die.'

Condon pondered this.

'What did you find in my hat?' he asked, knowing the answer.

'Two passports to Boot Hill,' she said bluntly. 'I burned them.'

Cliff digested this. 'The wanted posters, eh? Do you know those men?'

'Better than you do, or you would not be hunting that kind of bounty. Your welcome to the Massacre should convince you of their character.'

'The Massacre?'

'The name of Vern Gregory's ranch.'

'A grim name for a spread.'

'It has a reason. A party of white settlers got lost up here years ago, and were

10

massacred by a tribe of Apaches. It's been called Massacre Flat since. I don't want you to meet the same fate as the settlers.'

'I'd already have met it, except for you. I'd like a smoke.'

'Lucky your tobacco was in your left pocket.'

He heard her fumble in her dress and then awkwardly roll a cigarette. When she took a match from the tin box he always carried, he hoped to see her face, but she turned it from him as she struck the match and choked on the smoke. He saw the outlines of her throat and her cheek, brown and smooth but distorted by her efforts to get the cigarette going. She put the quirly between his lips.

'I wish I could see you,' he said.

'You would be disappointed.'

'Why should I be disappointed? You saved my life; that should make you beautiful to me. I can see you even in the dark. Your hair is like the sun, and your eyes as blue as the sky with stars in them. I can see the warm redness of your lips . . .'

A sob stopped him, and he felt a stab of guilt at his thoughtless recital.

'I'm ugly and stupid and coarse,' she said in a tight, pent-up voice. 'I'm not asking for lies and flattery. I want only to get you well and off the mesa before you are discovered. I can't take you to the ranch, because that would mean death for you and a beating for

11

me. I must nurse you here until you are able to ride. Don't make my job unbearable by mocking me.'

'Mocking you?' Cliff's hand reached for her arm, which she jerked away from him. 'I could never mock you. You are beautiful because you think beautiful, and act beautiful, you possess the beauty that counts. There is more to beauty than a face. Having all that beauty, how can you be ugly?'

'I've got to go,' she said tensely. 'I'll leave the dog to protect you.'

'Thanks; he's a beautiful animal. Is he yours?'

'Vern Gregory doesn't think so. I left more food for you. I've got to get back to the ranch before Emma misses me or Gust Allen becomes suspicious. I'll see you tomorrow.'

'Before dark?'

'I don't know.' She faded into the shadows.

She didn't come in the daylight. For four or more nights she came in the darkness, feeding him, changing the bandage, and helping him in every necessary way. On the fifth day, Cliff felt the fever returning, and the grim specter of infection haunted him. In spite of Naomi's ministrations, a warren in the brush was no place for a wound to heal.

That day she came in the daylight, dressed in fringed buckskin pants, moccasins and a flannel shirt. At first Cliff thought she was another figment of his fevered imagination,

12

but the truth was brought home to him by her appearance. For a moment guilt shamed him as he realized the cruelty of his description of her the first night he had spoken to her. She was not golden, her eyes were not blue, there were no stars in them. Instead, her dark hair was drawn back, flaunting a yellow bow clumsily tied. Her eyes were brown, and the blacking she had streaked on her brows accentuated their depth and sadness. She had smeared rouge on her cheeks, and her reddened lips made a livid gash of her honest mouth. She stood before him, her chin up as though to say, 'Look at me. Am I not beautiful, just as you said?'

It was true he had not expected her to be so plain, but her desperate attempt to acquire the glamour he had so innocently attributed to her struck him as a ghastly joke. He forced a smile, trying to keep pity from it. She saved him the necessity of comment by exclaiming:

'They suspect you're here alive. Ace Longest found your horse and brought it to the ranch, and Vern Gregory questioned me. Even my mother is curious. You've got to get away.'

Cliff closed his eyes, and the fever was a torment. 'Forget about me,' he said gruffly. 'You've done what you could. I'll have to make it on my own.'

'Your fever's up,' she said, kneeling beside him.

13

'Infection. You should have let me die.'

'Coward's talk. Wait here.'

Naomi returned leading a cow pony with a bedroll and a canteen tied to the worn saddle.

'I couldn't bring your horse; Ace claims him. You'll have to use mine,' she said urgently.

'Do you think I'd leave without Bolo—my horse?'

'If you want to live. You can come back. Hurry.'

Cliff struggled to his feet and stood swaying, whipped by fever. Then a low, husky voice spoke behind the girl, and another girl stepped from the trees.

'There is no need to hurry, Naomi.'

Naomi spun around as though slapped, and gasped, 'Maxine! What are you doing here?'

Condon stared at the strange girl with ill-disguised curiosity. This was the girl he had described. Where Naomi was plain and shy, Maxine was golden, vital, utterly lovely. It was she who had the golden hair, the flawless skin just touched with tan, and blue eyes which could be bold and soft by turns. She wore a spotless divided skirt of soft doeskin and decorated boots without a scuff mark on them. The green silk shirt was a frame for her beauty, topped by a pure white scarf that fluttered from her throat. Her flat-crowned sombrero of beaver hung from its cord down her back, and the sun struck

14

fire in her golden hair.

'Since when have you the right to question me?' Maxine asked in a voice slightly tinged with pity. 'When I found you had been using my cosmetics while you pretended to clean my room, I decided to follow you. I suspected something unusual had come into your life, and I remembered hearing about a trespasser on the south boundary. I see I was right. Give this cowboy a shave and a haircut, and he'd be right handsome. You couldn't be Carl Gabler, rep for Kile coming up from Mescosa?'

Cliff's mind worked fast. Stalling for time, he lied:

'Kile told me to use the south trail; less likely to run into lawmen. I didn't expect to get shot at.'

'The boundary is posted,' Maxine said flatly. Then she turned to Naomi. 'Get that paint off your face; you look hideous.'

'You look good and kind and honest, Naomi,' Cliff said, resenting Maxine's words. 'You've got a charm the years can't take away. Don't let her hurt you.'

'Hurt her? You fool! I'm being kind to her. She will only hurt herself more by getting such notions. We can't stand here and talk; you're a sick man. We've got to get you to the ranch.'

'You'll get him killed, Maxine,' Naomi warned.

15

'Do you want him to die here in this rabbit warren, Naomi? If he's Carl Gabler, Vern will want to see him. You go ahead, Naomi. Bring a buckboard to the south road, and bring Patch with you. We'll meet you there. This cowboy isn't going to make it very far.'

Naomi scrubbed her face with the cloth she had meant to use to bathe Cliff, and without a word mounted the horse she had brought for him and rode silently away.

Maxine's beautiful face was drifting before his bleary eyes, and they were alone.

'Come on. You can get into my saddle; I'll ride behind,' Maxine said, gripping his arm and leading him into the trees. She took his chaps along. How he got into the saddle he wasn't sure. He grasped the pommel with his left hand and somehow heaved himself into the leather. Maxine hung the chaps and gunbelt over the pommel, and with a lithe movement she was up behind him, her gloved hand reaching for the reins. After that there was a period of swaying movement, periods of darkness alternating with periods of furious pain when he was conscious of the girl's arms around him, steadying him in the saddle. Finally he practically fell from the saddle and lay on the grass beside the ruts of a wagon road.

Maxine took a raincoat from behind her saddle and pillowed his head. Then she opened the canteen, splashed water in his face and let it trickle through his lips. Revived

16

momentarily, Cliff looked up into her blue eyes.

'I'm beholden to you and your sister,' he mumbled through fever-cracked lips.

'My sister?' Maxine exclaimed. 'Whatever gave you the idea she was my sister? She and her mother work for me in the house. Their name is Beyer.'

'You mean they work for your mother?'

'I have no mother. I'm mistress of the house.'

Cliff lay with his eyes closed, pondering this. The mistress of Massacre—a grim title. He drifted off, the words echoing in his mind. When his mind was lucid again, he opened his eyes. She was still seated beside him, and when she saw he was conscious, she said, 'I hope you have papers, Carl, proving your identity.'

Cliff's mind groped for the right answer.

'They were in a round metal tube attached to my saddle,' he lied.

'And the money?'

Of course there would be money involved.

'It was in the can with my papers.'

'How much?'

Was she testing him? 'Kile never told me how much. He put the papers and the money in the can and sealed it. I never ask questions, and answer only the ones I have to.'

'There was no can on your saddle,' she accused him.

'Then it got torn off in the brush. Who brought my horse in?'

'Ace Longest.'

'Ask him about the can,' Cliff said suggestively.

'And get a bullet in return?'

'There's no bullet for one as beautiful as you, Maxine.'

It was true. There would be no bullet for her. Ace Longest loved her.

'Ace would not steal from us,' she said.

'You mean there's honor among thieves?'

'I resent that! How dare you come here calling us thieves, when we're trying to save your life?'

Her profile was turned toward him, and Cliff marveled at its perfection.

'My life isn't saved yet, Max,' he said, using the familiar form of her name.

'If you're Carl Gabler, you're safe enough.'

'And if I'm not?'

Her small chin set stubbornly, and she did not reply.

Cliff closed his eyes and let the languor wash over him. He began to suspect that he was going to die, and with a lie on his lips.

The buckboard came before the sun went down. Cliff felt himself being lifted; opening his eyes, he looked up into a black face with a patch over one eye.

'Let me help you, Patch,' he heard Naomi say.

18

A soft voice drawled, 'Lawsy, no, Miss Naomi. Ah can handle him easy.' A row of snow-white teeth showed through the grinning lips.

CHAPTER TWO

The jolting of the buckboard stopped, and Cliff opened his feverish eyes. Above him, the leafy boughs of cottonwoods intertwined, and he could smell the perfume of flowers. Turning his head, he saw the skinned white pine poles supporting the porch of a big house. At first he couldn't see the people, but he could hear their voices.

'Ace had no right to shoot him in the back,' Naomi's voice said. 'That's why I tried to save him.'

'I was only following your orders, Mister Gregory,' a flat, toneless voice said. 'You said, anybody who crosses the deadline, kill them.' Then with a flash of anger, 'But I didn't shoot him in the back!'

'You shot to kill.'

'I gave a warning.'

'A shout in the dark with a bullet on its heels,' Naomi said.

'Shut up, Naomi,' Maxine said. 'It's a good thing you didn't kill him, Ace. He claims to be Carl Gabler, the rep from Kile.'

A short silence followed her revelation. Half opening his eyes, Cliff twisted his head until he could see the group near the porch steps. There was a tall man, half bald, with colorless, hooded eyes, an aristocratic nose and a mouth that chewed upon a cold cigar. He wore a broadcloth coat, a silk shirt with a string tie, and riding breeches with English style boots. It was an outfit normally worn by strangers and dudes, but this man was neither. He had the arrogance of a man who has his way, the cold expression of a man who does not care how he gets it. This had to be Vern Gregory.

Gregory addressed the man called Ace, a dark man with a thin, pointed face and a nose too large for his slit of a mouth. The opaque eyes that straddled the big nose had the piercing stare of a snake, and the short stiff hair accentuated the oversized ears. A face on one of the posters.

'Longest, you've got a ready gun, but the judgment of a two-year-old steer. We can't take any chances at this stage of the game. We could have handled the man here.'

'Your orders, Mister Gregory—shoot to kill if they cross the deadline.'

'But you didn't kill, thank God. This could have tangled up the deal we've been sweating out for all these months. Help Gust Allen bring him into the house.'

The big Negro with the patch over his eye protested, 'Reckon Ah cain handle him mahself, boss. He ain't no heavier than a yearling.'

'He's hurt badly, Patch. Be careful with him,' Maxine said.

Then Cliff saw, through half shut eyes, the woman standing near Vern Gregory. Her dark hair was hacked off at the nape of her neck and brushed from her square, high-boned face. Her eyes were expressionless, but they looked as though they were on the verge of kindness, a kindness she kept in check. She was short, but solidly built; Naomi, standing near her, was a good two inches taller. There was a resemblance between them, although the older woman's hair was laced with the first streaks of gray. He knew she was Emma Beyer, Naomi's mother.

'Take him to my place,' Emma said. 'I'll have to tend him. No sense me running back and forth up here.'

'We'll do nothing of the kind,' Maxine said imperiously. 'Bring him in the house, Patch.'

'You got a personal interest in him, Maxine?' Emma asked, her gray eyes fixed on the girl.

'Don't be impertinent, Emma! You stick to your housework; that's what you get paid for.'

A change came over Vern Gregory's face;

the hooded eyes darted like mice, and his mouth slackened when he removed his cigar. There was a hidden weakness there it was hard to define. He ran his tongue along his lips before he spoke.

'Do as Emma says, Gust,' he said to the big negro.

Maxine flared, 'What do you mean, letting a scrub-woman have her way? I want him here in the house.'

'Shut up, Max!' Vern Gregory said with controlled fury. His fury was out of character. The look that passed between father and daughter was one of pure hate.

'Drive him down, Patch, and bring him inside,' Emma said.

'You've got no place for him,' Maxine insisted.

'I'll make a place.'

The buckboard moved on and stopped before a modest log cabin set back in a yard of flowers and shrubs. Cliff was awed by the ease and gentleness with which the big Negro moved him. Inside, Emma led the way. Cliff caught a glimpse of a big room which was used for cooking, eating and general living. There were a couple of doors at the rear, and one at the end through which he was carried.

'Put him on my bed, Patch.' Then she turned to Naomi, who had followed them. 'Get me some hot water, lots of it. Tear up some of the flour sacks I've been saving.

Then go out and get me some of that herb growing at the end of the vegetable garden.'

Emma went efficiently to work, unwinding the bandages, cutting away part of his flannel shirt so she could remove it over his left arm. Vaguely he remembered his badge, but she threw the shirt aside without searching it. When Patch came with the hot water, she spoke to Condon in her slow, patient voice.

'Can you hear me?'

To Condon, the words came from a long way off down a funnel of pain. He moved his head. The solemn, strong face of the woman swam before his half-opened eyes.

'I'd give you a slug of whiskey, hombre, but it wouldn't do you no good. It would drive the poison faster through your blood. This is going to hurt real bad. Pray God you pass out fast.'

He hadn't the will to respond. His thoughts were wiped out by the inferno of pain that sucked him into oblivion as Emma pulled the stuck bandages from the festering wound.

She worked with efficient hands, which she had washed with whiskey, lancing the angry wound to let the vile fluid spew forth. Thankful that her patient was unconscious, she pressed and swabbed the wound, cutting away the putrid flesh, staunching the blood with cloths wrung out in scalding water. Her plain face was drawn and intent until she had extracted the bullet and had the flesh cleansed

23

and sterile.

'I put the herbs in the boiling water on the stove, Ma, and put in a fork to boil with them,' Naomi said, watching the operation. She had seen her mother brand a steer, slit an ear on a dogie, and doctor a calf with the same precision.

'Bring them in the pot; don't touch them with your hands.'

Fishing the brown mass from the water with the fork, unmindful of the scalding heat, Emma fashioned a poultice upon the wound, and bound it with the boiled strips of flour sacking.

'Twelve hours more and you could have buried him,' she said laconically.

'I didn't know. I tried . . .'

'There's a saying, Naomi, that the road to hell is paved with good intentions. I reckon it's true. I *know*. You should have brung him here in the first place.'

'I was afraid to, Ma. He's good; you can tell by looking at his face. I didn't want him to come here so they could finish the job. I wanted to get him well and send him back off the hill. I would have gone with him if he'd have me, away from Massacre forever.'

'Things will work out,' Emma said. 'If he's Carl Gabler, like he says, there's nothing to worry about.'

'And if he's not?'

'Do you think I like all this killing, Naomi?

There's some things get started that a person can't stop. There'll be a showdown soon, that'll either make or break the Massacre.'

'In the meantime people cheat, and steal and die. It's like killing wild hogs to shoot a man without giving him a chance.'

'Amen to that.'

'You could talk to Vern Gregory and that beautiful daughter of his. Sometimes he listens to you.'

'Why should he listen to me?'

'I don't know, but he does. If this man dies, something good, something great will die with him.'

'Naomi,' Emma said patiently, 'if we were all great, there would be no use for greatness. If we were all beautiful, there would be no need for beauty. I ain't so sure but that meanness and ugliness have a purpose, even if it's only to nurture greatness and enhance beauty.'

'Carl Gabler doesn't look like the kind of man who would work for Kile,' Naomi said.

'He ain't Carl Gabler,' Emma said flatly.

Naomi looked up quickly, a question in her brown eyes. 'But his initials are punched into his hat band. I saw them when I took out—took out—'

'When you took out what?'

'Nothing. I just saw the initials, C.G.'

'What did you take out of his hat band? You near let him die trying to protect him,

25

child. If he's in danger, there ain't much you can do about it alone. You'd better tell me everything.'

'What makes you think you can save him? We're only scrub-women, you and me—you heard Maxine. We're dirt to her and Vern Gregory. I won't wear her cast-off clothes, and she hates me for that.'

'They're better than most.'

'Only because she can't stand a run-down boot heel or soiled doeskin. When I get a chance, I take her clothes to the Mission and let the padres give them to the Indians. I'm more comfortable in my buckskin pants and Indian shoes.'

'We're getting off the track. What did you find in his hat?'

'Will you promise to keep it a secret, at least until he can speak for himself?'

'I don't bray like a jackass, Naomi, you know that.'

'I found two wanted posters.'

'Massacre men?'

'Ace Longest, and another one I don't know.'

'This man resembles somebody. I ain't sure—a man came in with the last bunch of cattle Vern Gregory bought. Let's see his hat.'

Naomi brought the hat from the chair near the living room door, where she had dropped it along with his chaps and gunbelt after bringing them in from the buckboard.

'There it is, C.G.,' she pointed out.

Emma studied the hat band and shook her head. 'That ain't a C.G., child; that's a C.C. Now what did you do with the posters?'

'I burned them.'

'You what?'

'I burned them.'

'I wish you hadn't. But never mind that now. Get this mess cleaned up and stay with him. I'll give you a hand with that blanket. We'll try to slip a clean one under him before he comes to.'

When the blanket was changed, Emma left, and Naomi scrubbed and scoured the rough wooden floor. She took his shirt and, starting to wash it, found the star badge pinned inside. She read the wording on it: 'Official Representative, Delgado Cattlemen's Ass'n.' Thoughtfully she pinned the badge inside her own shirt and felt the coldness of it against her heart.

The room was getting dark, and Naomi lit the oil lamp to drive back the darkness. To her surprise, there was a knock on the door, and when she opened it, Gust Allen stood there, hat in hand, his huge body filling the door frame.

'Come in, Patch,' she said cordially.

The big Negro entered. There was a smile on his friendly face, showing his strong white teeth.

27

'Emma sent me, chile; she reckoned you-all might need a hand undressin' him. Cain't let him waller in them dirty clothes no mo'. I brung these that Emma gave me.'

Out of his hat, Patch drew some rolled up underwear, evidently some of Gregory's.

'He's still unconscious, Patch.'

'Better so. Ah'll handle him easy as an angel, chile. You-all get me some wash-cloths and a towel and some of that warm water. Ah'll light me a lamp in the bedroom.'

After providing the necessities, Naomi paced the living room while Patch eased off Cliff's stiff California pants and removed his drawers, which were stained with the blood that had run down his side. Then he bathed him gently with the warm water, and though Cliff groaned once or twice, he seemed to relax under the dark man's ministrations. Putting on the fine cashmere underwear Emma had sent, Patch covered him up and returned to the living room.

'How is he, Patch?' Naomi asked quickly.

'Ah reckon his fever is about to break, chile. Emma knows how to doctor a gunshot wound—she's seen plenty of them. Ain't no man going to die with a purty nurse lak' you-all to tend him.'

Ignoring the compliment as a kindness undeserved, Naomi said, 'If he does live—what then, Patch?'

Patch scratched his head. 'Ah reckon it all

28

depends on what kind of a man he is. If he is a rep fo' Mistah Kile, he ain't got no worry.'

'But if he isn't? If he's a stranger—if he just wandered up here by accident?'

'Ain't nobody wanderin' up from the south end by accident.'

'If he was a lawman or bounty hunter, what then, Patch?'

'Jes you-all pray he ain't none of them, chile. Mistah Gregory don't cotton none to snoopers. Ace only acted on his orders. Them bordah signs read: 'Deadline, Massacre. No trespassing!'

'It was dark; he couldn't read the sign.'

'Ah looked at that man, and I says to mahself, heah's a man won't stop easy. He's got a stubborn chin, with a cleft in it. For a young man, he's done mo' than a mite of living. You-all can tell by the lines in his face. Be a shame if he ended up heah.'

'Isn't there something we can do to help him—at least until he gets his strength back?'

'You-all can get him a horse, when he's able to ride, and send him away in the dead of night.'

CHAPTER THREE

When Cliff Condon regained consciousness, it was with a distinct feeling of well-being.

29

There was still a taut soreness on his right side, but the fever had broken twenty-four hours before, and the relief was so great he regarded the hurt of his wound impersonally. He was aware of the cashmere underwear and the clean blankets, and bits of memory made a pattern in his mind. He remembered being brought to the strange bed, trundled like a child in the big Negro's arms. He remembered the older woman tearing loose the blood-caked bandages on his side, and there memory ended.

He stared up into the dim light and wondered if it were morning or evening. He made out the form of the girl sitting in the chair at the foot of the bed, keeping a silent vigil, and the vision of Naomi, her face distorted with cosmetics, haunted him. He owed this girl more than he could ever repay, and her continued loyalty added to the debt. He didn't move, unsure what to do. Then he heard voices coming through the half-opened door.

'I can't take a chance on him spoiling things now,' Vern Gregory's cultured, deep voice said.

'But if he is Carl Gabler, nothing will be changed,' Emma said.

'What makes you think he's Carl Gabler?'

'His initials were punched in the sweat band of his hat.'

'Let me see it.'

30

There was a pause, and then Gregory said in an uncertain tone, 'It's a C.G., all right.'

Cliff frowned. Somebody must have made the last C look like a G. It would be a simple thing to do; even the tine of a fork would suffice.

'He was delirious,' Emma said; 'he raved about a letter Kile was sending.'

That had to be a lie. He may have been delirious and he might have said things, but not about a letter from Kile, because he knew nothing of such a letter.

'Kile was supposed to send a letter,' Gregory agreed. 'But this man spoke of papers and money he had with him in a metal tube. There was no metal tube on his saddle.'

'Who found his horse?'

'Ace Longest.'

'Did you ask him if he kept it for himself? He could destroy the papers, keep the money, and kill Carl Gabler to keep his mouth shut. Why don't you ask him?'

'Because I'm not ready to die. Ace is a handy tool to have around. Some day I'll kill him.'

'I didn't figure you to be easily scared,' Emma said boldly.

'I've got to question the wounded man, Emma. If he's not Gabler, there may be others who'll follow him.'

'You think he'd tell you if there was?'

'As you well know, there are ways to make

31

people talk.'

'Not in my house,' Emma said.

There was an authority in her voice that disturbed Condon. What secret did she hold over Gregory to make her immune from his cold authority?

'I'll be back, when he's able to be moved, to take him up to my house. Nothing is going to endanger my plan, so near completion. Do you hear that? Nothing!' Gregory said heatedly.

Condon felt like an animal in a trap. His ruse about the tin cylinder containing papers and money would soon be disproved, and before that happened he had to make some kind of plan. The mention of a letter coming from Kile gave him another straw to hang onto. Dared he continue to impersonate the man called Gabler? The subterfuge might buy him time to understand more of the plot being planned here on the Massacre. He still had five hundred head of cattle to find, and two men to bring back to face the law. Ace Longest was one of those men. He still had to find the other. He had to find his brother Arny, too. Could he have been murdered as Hal Chester had been?

Hearing Emma go out of the house, he looked at the figure sitting patiently near the foot of the bed and said softly, 'Is that you, Naomi?'

The girl moved quickly to his side, her

hand pressing upon his forehead.

'Your fever's gone. My prayers were answered. How do you feel?' Her hand lingered upon him.

'Like I just got out of the fire. I heard them talking in there—I hope I don't step into the frying pan,' he paraphrased the old saying. 'I need a friend, Naomi.'

'I've never had a friend,' she said, 'a real friend. At the Mission school in Kaibito, I made friends with the Navajo kids, but they went back to their tribes.'

'Let me be your friend,' Cliff said. 'Trust me.'

'I'd like that, Carl Gabler.'

He knew she was questioning him purposely. He noticed her hesitation. 'Believe that I am Carl Gabler. We all have secrets, Naomi, things locked up inside up like animals in cages, struggling to break out. Sometimes these things must be kept caged, lest they break out too soon and destroy us.'

'I know,' she said softly. 'Until I touched you, I was only half alive, but you have awakened the other half. If you should die, I would die, Carl.' She used the name naturally. 'I washed your shirt and mended it.'

He waited for her to go on, but she made no mention of the star badge. She walked across the room with a firm, even step and brought the shirt to him. It was now too dark to see the shirt, but his fingers told him the badge was gone.

'If they found a badge or wanted posters on you,' she said pointedly, 'they would kill you. Until now I've never bothered myself about the things Vern Gregory did, and I took Maxine's abuse because I understood the devils that drove her. All that beauty and talent and education, without a heart to make it worth-while. She's been taught everything but love and charity. I hope some day she finds them before she turns into a bitter old crone. My own mother is almost a stranger to me. If she has reasons for the thing she does, I don't know what they are. Outside of living at the Mission school, where I learned to read and write because Emma insisted on it, I've seen little of the world. Once she took me to St. George, where she went on some business, and before we got there we passed Brigham Young's winter home where he lived when it was too cold in Salt Lake. We saw him in a carriage with his favorite wife. I remember thinking how beautiful she was and how pretty her clothes were. I guess I dreamed of being like that some day, so I lived in a make-believe world. But now that world is deserting me.'

'You'll find your dream, Naomi, because you're strong and kind,' he said.

'I've got some food on the stove. You've got to eat it to give you strength. Then get all

34

the sleep you can, and by tomorrow night maybe we can get you away from here.'

'I can't leave the Massacre without doing the job I came to do.'

'I've got a place where you can hide and grow strong.'

After eating the food she brought in, Condon felt a stupor come over him, induced by his weakness and the comfort of a full stomach. He thought about his star badge and decided to let her keep it for now.

When next he awoke, he was startled by the shaft of sunlight slanting across his bed. For the first time since he had been shot, his mind felt clear and his body eager for action.

The door creaked open, and he looked up, expecting to see Naomi or Emma coming in to check on him. Instead, two men in Levis and sweat-stained shirts, with chiseled, sun-whipped faces, slid quietly into the room. The one was as lean as a pole, and slightly bent at the shoulders as though continually dodging. The other was thick and heavy, but not fat, with swarthy skin and pale eyes. He had a scar on his neck, and his trigger finger was missing.

'Who are you?' Cliff inquired, tensing.

'I'm Colt Denger,' the thick man said, 'ramrod of this outfit.' He jerked his head at the other man, who had a knife thrust into his belt. 'This is Mex Embozo; he don't talk much. Gregory wants to see you. We come to

35

help you up to the big house.'

Cliff frowned. 'I'm not in very good shape. What's his hurry?'

'He don't cotton to the idea of you sloping off.'

'Why should I slope off?'

'Gregory's a careful man. He ain't taking no chances. Reckon we can carry you if you can't walk.'

To resist was useless. He wondered where Emma and Naomi were or whether they had purposely let these men in the house. Under the blankets, he tested his muscles, and they responded, but with little strength. Throwing back the covers, Condon swung his feet to the floor and saw the questioning looks of the two men at his cashmere underwear.

'Borrowed,' he said laconically. 'Give me my pants. I reckon I can walk.'

His pants, as well as his shirt, had been washed, and he wondered whom he had to thank for that. Denger, with the movements of a man unused to doing personal favors for others, helped him on with his boots. Clutching the wooden headboard of the bed, he rose unsteadily. A wave of weakness threatened to down him, and he winced at the pain in his side. Fighting for control, he steadied himself.

'Give me an arm, Embozo, and I'll manage,' he said with more bravado than he felt.

The Mexican, his long, stooped body moving with exceptional grace, extended his arm as gallantly as though escorting a woman. Denger picked up Cliff's hat and put it on his head. His confidence grew with each step, and he realized his disability was confined to the area of the wound itself.

Pulling himself to the seat of the buckboard with his left hand, he waited for Denger to pick up the reins. Embozo mounted a beautiful golden horse, with a silver-mounted saddle, champed on a silver bit, and a silver-conchoed martingale reaching back between his long legs. The Mexican and his horse made an impressive picture. Condon thought of his own horse and wondered how he was going to get him back.

Condon braced himself against the jerk of the wagon as it started, and steadied his wounded shoulder with his left hand. The sun was bright, and he took in his surroundings with a sweeping glance. The ranch was built in a shallow basin, in the bottom of which sparkled the water of a large pond. There were quaking aspen and cottonwoods surrounding the pond, and in the grove of trees rose the big house to which he had been taken on his arrival. As nearly as a house of peeled white pine logs can, it resembled a Southern mansion, with its high porch supported by tall pine poles. The whole edifice had been white-washed, but it made an imposing appearance out there on the edge of nowhere. Beyond a stone wall stood the barns and sheds, surrounded by fences and corrals, and to one side was a long structure, evidently a bunk-house and cook shack. The whole setup was swallowed by the vast space of the mesa, as though it had been dropped in that isolated spot by a giant hand and then forgotten.

At the porch steps the wagon stopped, and dismounting with difficulty, Cliff steadied himself with a hand on the wheel before trusting his legs. But they responded adequately, and he mounted the four wide steps leading up to the porch without mishap. Once more he found the confidence of returning strength, and with Denger following close behind, he reached the front door. The plank door, studded with bolts, had a knocker made of a branding iron hanging in the center, and this struck a metal plate when it was swung. But he had no need to swing the knocker, because the door opened as though his arrival had been expected.

Condon, unused to silk and satin, was startled by the shining pink satin negligee in which Maxine greeted him. Lace made a white froth about her smooth throat, and ruffles swept the floor. He had come there expecting to meet Vern Gregory, with his enigmatic face and hooded eyes, or even Gust

38

Allen, his dark face gaping in a white smile, but he was unprepared for this vision.

Maxine's long hair had been braided, and it was wound about her head to make a golden crown above her bright blue eyes. Her long lashes and arched brows made her eyes look larger and deeper than they were, while red had been applied so subtly to cheeks and lips as to give the appearance of inner radiance. Her exciting perfume stirred his senses, and he stood in awestruck wonder for one awkward moment. He had seen pictures of fine women, and one or two paintings, but he had never expected to come face to face with one.

'What's the matter, Carl Gabler; have you never seen a woman before?' she said, holding out her hand.

'Not one so beautiful, ma'am.' He was supporting himself with his good arm against the door frame, so he didn't remove his hat.

'Rubbish! Just because I wash my face and comb my hair, that doesn't make me beautiful, Carl.'

'Then my eyes and nose are liars, ma'am.'

'You should get around more. In Denver I'm just an ordinary female.'

'Then Denver is overrun with beauty, ma'am.'

'Stop ma'aming me—you sound like a sheep. You know my name. Use it.'

Condon got over his first shock of surprise,

and realized Maxine had fixed herself up purposely to impress him.

'You *are* beautiful, Max, and you have the courage and brains to run such a ranch as this,' he said boldly.

Her eyes sharpened, and the lines of her mouth grew taut. 'Don't delude yourself, Carl. I'm mistress of the house; nothing more.'

'The mistress of Massacre,' he said musingly.

At this her temper flared. 'Don't call me that! I hate the Massacre, I hate this country, I hate the hills. I hate putting up with a scrub-woman and a half-wit girl for servants.'

'Then why do you stay?'

'My father is a domineering, cruel man.'

'It looks to me like he pampers you.'

A deep voice with the whip of authority in it demanded from a room leading off the hall, 'What's going on out there, Max. Bring Gabler in here, and keep your coquetry for more important game.'

Biting her lip, Maxine turned and led the way into a big room that evidently served as office and library. There was a big desk littered with papers and ledgers. A gun rack held oiled and polished guns. There were two bearskin rugs on the floor. The rawhide drapes at the windows had been drawn back, admitting shafts of sunlight in which dust atoms danced and swirled, and cobwebs festooned the corners of the ceiling.

'Forgive the filth,' Maxine said with a touch of sarcasm. 'He won't allow anyone to touch this room. He's afraid they'll stir up ghosts.'

'Enough of that, Max. Get out.'

Condon could almost feel the clash of wills as he studied father and daughter. Chin up, Maxine turned with a swish of her ruffles and went out, leaving Condon with Vern Gregory and Colt Denger.

Gregory, his cordovan boots polished like burnished copper, picked a quirt up off his desk and paced the floor, tapping the whip against his boot as he walked. Without looking directly at Condon, he talked.

'So you're Carl Gabler—at least that's what you say—but you have no proof.'

'I reckon only a fool carries a passport in this country, Gregory.' Pretending not to have heard the talk in the cabin, he continued, 'If you care to look in my hat band, my initials—'

'Never mind; I saw them. Emma thinks you're Gabler, but I can't take any chances on you being a ringer. How come you were riding on an unbranded horse?'

'I caught that horse wild and clean. He's never been marked, and God help the man who tries it.'

'Better tell Ace about that; he claims the horse. Ace has no scruples about marking

41

anything good and plain,' Gregory shrugged.

'Like he marked me?' Condon asked.

Gregory slithered his lean frame around on the balls of his feet and faced the ramrod seated on a rawhide couch.

'All right, Colt; is this the man you know?'

Condon felt the chill hand of danger. Colt Denger shook his bushy head. 'He ain't the man I know. Never did get his name straight, but he had straw hair, and half of one ear was bit off. I heard he was called Frenchy.'

Realizing the danger he was in, Condon's mind worked swiftly. He had been brought here to be exposed before Vern Gregory as an imposter, but Colt Denger was unsure of his evidence. Condon took a chance.

'Frenchy's dead. He made the mistake of holding out on Kile to fill his own pocket. Kile sent me because I wasn't known up this way, but he don't trust me overmuch. If you could find the metal tube with the papers and money, you could break the seal and open it. He said there was something in there to identify me.'

'Didn't Kile give you any idea when the barges would arrive?'

Condon was being fed scraps of information, and he wasn't sure whether this information was valid or whether he was being sucked into trapping himself. The less he volunteered, the better. If his real purpose on the Massacre became known, he would not live to see another sun.

'I reckon all that information will be in the letter, Gregory. The tube contained papers and money to clinch the deal.'

Gregory's hooded eyes looked at Cliff. Cliff stared back unwaveringly.

'There's no proof there was a tube,' Gregory said flatly.

'Did you ask Ace about it?'

'He denied finding a tube.'

'Do you believe him?'

'I'll let you accuse him of stealing it, Gabler.'

Here was an excuse to get out on the range alone, Condon realized. He needed proof that the cattle stolen from the Delgado range were actually on the Massacre, and a clue to the whereabouts of his missing brother.

'I'll find the tube myself. I know about where it could be lost—if it is still lost,' he offered casually.

'Good,' Gregory said. 'I'll send Ace Longest with you.'

Before Condon could recover from the shock of Gregory's remark, Maxine came back into the room. She still wore the pink negligee.

'Breakfast is ready, Vern. Emma says to come and get it or she'll throw it out. You'll be our guest, Carl Gabler.'

Colt Denger rose and headed for the door. 'I'll be getting to work. I et breakfast hours ago.'

'I don't aim to be a bother, either,' Condon said. 'I'll go to the cook shack for a hand-out.'

'You'll do nothing of the kind,' Maxine said. 'We eat breakfast later than the cowhands. They have to get out on the range early.'

Playing for time, Condon made no further remarks, but followed Maxine into the dining room, with Vern bringing up the rear. The dining room, in contrast to the library, was scrubbed and polished, and white linen covered the table. The furniture was made of native wood, rugged and comfortable. Seeing Condon's admiring glances, Gregory volunteered:

'I brought in some artisans from Mexico to build the furniture on the place—everything but the piano.'

'You have a piano?'

'Maxine will play for you sometime.'

'I'm afraid I'll have no time for concerts.'

'But you will,' Maxine assured him. 'I had Emma fix you up a room here in the house.'

'But I can't. I'm not used to this kind of living. I'll feel more at home in the bunkhouse,' Cliff protested.

'You'll stay here—at least until the barges arrive, or a letter of explanation comes. It will be safer that way,' Gregory said with finality.

Was he being held a prisoner, or was he being protected? Condon didn't know, and

44

for the moment there was nothing he could do about it. Patch, a white apron tied about his middle, came in with the food. The effect was incongruous, the big Negro wearing Levis, tucked into cowboy boots, playing butler. But then, everything he had so far learned about Massacre was incongruous. Patch put platters of side meat, eggs and hot cakes on the table, and greeted them with a smiling, 'Good mawnin'.'

Condon was amazed at his own appetite.

When the meal was over, he rose, feeling the beneficial effects of the meal on his body and spirit. He tried to think of a subterfuge that would let him get away by himself so he could do a little snooping.

'That meal sure did bring back my strength. Reckon a little riding will loosen me up. If I can get my horse I'll make a try at finding the metal tube.'

'Ace isn't here to go with you,' Gregory said flatly. 'Besides, he probably has your horse with him.'

Condon was trying to think up a retort to that when Maxine spoke.

'I'll go with him, Vern,' she said, giving her father a warning look. 'It wouldn't be very safe to turn the executioner and his victim out together on such short notice.'

'Are you picking him out for another of your whipping boys, Max? He might resist your charms—how will you feel then?'

'Call me man-bait if you wish,' she said sharply. 'You made me this way.'

'Go on; take him!' Gregory snapped.

'I'll go down to the corrals and find a horse,' Condon suggested, uncomfortable before this show of raw hatred.

'Never mind,' Maxine said. 'Patch can bring out horses, while I change my clothes.'

CHAPTER FOUR

Mounted on a Massacre horse, Condon rode beside Maxine toward the southeastern rim of the mesa. Her horse was a silver gray with white tail and mane, which she called Silver. The brass conchas on her saddle were polished until they glowed, and there was a silver name plate mounted on the top of the horn. The horse they had furnished Cliff with was adequate, a sturdy cow pony, uncomplaining and responsible, but he was no Bolo. To his surprise, they had brought him his own saddle, which sported no metal to catch the sun and signal his whereabouts.

They rode past groups of cattle grazing, and Condon tried to ascertain if they were cattle he might know, but this was impossible. They skirted close enough to one group so that the brands were decipherable, and Condon pulled his horse to study them.

'That's the Massacre's brand,' Maxine informed him. 'A tomahawk. What could be more appropriate?'

It was a tomahawk, all right, complete with tassel. 'But they're not the same, the brands; the handle of the tomahawk points in different directions.'

'One of my intelligent father's foibles. According to him, the position of the handle tells what year the cow was born, and when it is old enough to sell.'

'A Western cowman needs no such sign to judge a beef,' Condon said. The explanation was logical enough, but such a brand could be used to change or plot out any other brand. The candle could blot out lines, the head could blot out circles, and the tassel could take care of other things.

'My father is not a Western cowman. He's a Southern gentleman, used to having money, and determined to have more. Sometimes I think he's taking revenge on the land itself.' She said this last with the same bitterness.

'Why do you say that?' He was becoming aware of the complexity of this girl, who, for some reason, was being educated, groomed and polished into a lady.

When she spoke next, it was as though she was bridging a gulf between them. 'According to my father, we were part of the lost party who were massacred here.'

Condon caught his breath. The news was a

47

distinct shock to him, and he exclaimed with feeling, 'How horrible!'

'I suppose it was.'

'But you were saved—and he was saved.'

'My mother hid me under her dresses. I was an infant. She lay upon me, and when they killed and scalped her they didn't find me. If they had, I'd be a young squaw now instead of a fine lady.'

'And your father, what about him?'

'He had gone on ahead to find a way out of the trap we had drifted into. When he came back, everybody was dead but me.'

Condon digested the horror of this. 'Then you don't even remember your mother?'

'He says she was beautiful, that I take after her. I suppose he has reason for his bitterness, and he has made me part of his revenge on the Yankees, and the Apaches, and this high, brooding land. He thinks he's a god and can recreate my mother through me. Perhaps he can—if he can sell me to the right man.'

'Sell you?'

'What else will it be? Love has no cash value; it's not like wealth and position. He means to get them for me and bask in my success. I'll get my satisfaction out of it; my time will come.'

Condon was in a quandary. This fantastic story she had told him could be true, or it could be a monstrous fraud. He asked, 'Is all

48

this real—is it true? Have you any proof?'

'There was a massacre, all right; the remains of it can still be found at the foot of Mount Diablo. There were no witnesses.'

'What about Patch, he must have been there, if he came from Virginia with your father?'

'My father and Patch, who was but a boy then, got separated in Denver. Patch didn't find us again until after the massacre, when my father had decided to build the ranch here. Patch will tell you the same thing. What's the matter? You look skeptical. Do you doubt the story?'

'I don't doubt it, really; it's just too horrible to believe.'

'Well, believe it, and forget it.'

The finality of her tone erected a wall of silence between them as they rode to the ride of the Arroyo Diablo, where Condon had entered the Massacre. He stopped on the trail which led back from the brink of the cliff and looked around. 'I was shot right about here. Which way my horse bolted, I don't know.'

'It shouldn't be hard to find the tracks of a bolting horse,' she said, swinging gracefully to the ground.

Because mounting and dismounting were painful, Condon followed more slowly. Their eyes fixed on the ground, they searched among the grass and brush for telltale tracks. Neither of them saw a man ride out of the trees and sit staring at them. Maxine's Silver broke the silence with a warning snort, and Condon spun around to face Ace Longest.

The eyes under the warped hat were glowing coals of hatred and jealousy, and the slit of a mouth clamped on a cold cigarette.

'What are you doing here, Ace?' Maxine asked. 'You're supposed to be out on the range.'

'I reckon this is part of the range, ain't it?' Ace's voice was flat and cold.

'There is no work for you here,' she retorted.

'You're wrong, Miss Maxine. It's been hinted I stole a tin tube with papers and money in it. I came to look for that tube.'

Condon stood stiff and helpless. He had not bothered to wear his gun, because it would have been useless. There was death in Ace Longest's eyes, and Condon shuddered to think what would have happened had he come there alone. He wondered why Ace was not riding Bolo.

'Did you find the tube, Ace?' Maxine asked, approaching him.

'I got a notion there ain't no tube.'

'What makes you say that?'

'I checked Gabler's saddle. None of the latigoes were torn off,' Ace said. 'He's riding his saddle there; you can check it yourself.'

'The tube had a strap on it; it was hanging to my saddle horn,' Condon said, knowing

50

how shallow the explanation sounded. 'The strap must have broke.'

Maxine had reached Ace's side and stood looking up at him. Her shoulders were stiff, and her hands gripped the fringe of her skirt.

'If we don't find the tube, Ace, it doesn't mean you stole it. It could have rolled into a badger hole, down a cutbank and over the edge of the cliff. I know you wouldn't steal it; you've proved that by coming here to look for it. Now go about your work, and next time I go to Hanker, I'll let you take me.'

Somehow she managed a smile and, coupled with the appeal in her blue eyes, it struck a responsive chord in Ace Longest. Miraculously, his eyes softened and his face relaxed. He stared at her as though devouring her beauty and slowly straightened in the saddle. As he turned to go, he glared at Condon, but he spoke to Maxine.

'If he lays a hand on you—'

Condon watched the lean man ride away, and not until the sound of his horse had died did he say, 'I'm sorry, Max.'

'What for?'

'Because you had to humble yourself before that animal.'

'All animals have redeeming features, Carl. Some day I might need Ace Longest to protect me.'

'He'll expect a reward.'

'I'll give him a pat on the head.'

'He won't be satisfied with that.'

'Why should you worry? I've told you what my life's going to be. Now let's look for that phantom tube.'

As they mounted, Condon pondered her last remark; her words indicated that her belief in the missing tube was none too staunch. He had to go through the motions of looking for it, and when they found the trail on which Ace Longest had come, they followed it, examining every possible hiding place, until they reached the spot where Cliff had lain wounded and nearly dead. Of course, there was no tube.

'It could have been torn off after I fell off my horse,' he said lamely.

'We can go no farther today; it will take the whole afternoon to get home. Shall we stop here?'

'Stop?'

'I've got some jerky and sandwiches in my saddle bag. You may be able to ride all day without eating, but not me.'

Condon looked at the spot where the stains of his blood still darkened the ground. It could have been his grave, the resting place of his bones after the buzzards had stripped them.

'We can eat while riding back,' he said.

★　　★　　★

After dinner at the ranch, Patch led Condon to a room on the second floor at the rear of the house, away from the porch. They are making sure he stayed out. Patch, carrying a lamp, went into the room and put the lamp on the commode.

'Naomi, she fix up this room, suh. Made up a nice fresh bed and laid out a night shirt. You'll be right comfortable,' Patch said cheerfully.

When the Negro had gone, Condon paced the floor after removing his boots. His stockinged feet made no sound. He was dead tired and his shoulder was bone sore, yet he marveled at how much stronger he had become. Tired as he was, he could feel the strength returning to his side. He moved his arm tentatively, winced at the pain, but it obeyed his nerves.

He threw himself on the bed, still wearing his Levis and patched shirt. But when he lowered his head on the smooth, inviting pillow, he felt something stiff inside the pillowcase, that crackled as he moved. Curious, he reached inside the covering and drew out a note. He had turned the lamp down low, but there was enough light to read by. The note read:

'Carl: Do not go to sleep. You have got to leave the house tonight. I know you are not Carl Gabler or you would not have the

53

wanted posters and the badge. When Emma comes with the mail it will be too late. Naomi.'

She had left the note when she had made up his room. There was nothing he could do now but trust her. Quietly he pulled his boots on.

When Naomi came she did not knock, but slipped quietly into the room. For the first time he saw her in a skirt, a long skirt that reached to her shoe tops. She also wore a denim jacket that was too large for her. Her hair was drawn up under a bandana that was tied under her chin. Her soft face was turned up to him, and her brown eyes were alive with urgency. She was carrying towels draped across her arm, under which was concealed her left hand.

'There's no time for questions. Just listen to me and do as I tell you.'

She put the towels on the commode and revealed a gun held in the hand that had been hidden by them. Laying the gun down, she reached around and unhooked her skirt, letting it fall to the floor. Condon stood, spellbound by her swift actions. Under her skirt she was wearing another similar skirt. She removed the denim jacket, and from the pocket she withdrew another bandana.

'Put on the skirt; hang it low so it covers your boots. This jacket should fit you, though it might be snug. Tie this bandana around your head.'

Condon did as she instructed, suddenly realizing what her intentions were.

'If I do get out of here in this disguise, what will *you* do?'

'I'll manage.'

'Did anybody see you come here?'

'There's a guard outside, but he didn't bother me. I have a right here. Patch was half asleep in the dining room; but I told him I had forgotten your towels. He offered to bring them up himself, but I insisted on doing it. I don't know whether he suspected anything or not. I came in through the kitchen. You go through the dining room and out the front door. Stoop over a little so you won't look so tall. If there is a guard at the front of the house, ignore him and go straight down to Emma's cabin. You'll find a horse in the shed at the back, all saddled up. You can take off the skirt and ride south about a mile to the first grove of juniper. Wait for me there.'

He wanted to remonstrate, to refuse to let this girl put her life in danger to protect him, but he knew she had outlined the only course he could follow.

'Hide the gun in your skirt,' she warned him. 'Now go, not too quietly. I might have been heard coming here; they must hear me leaving.'

'Somehow, Naomi, I'll repay you,' he said, and brushed her forehead with his lips.

He edged into the hall, feeling strange and awkward in the long skirt and the bandana. He crouched a little as he moved down the stairs, hearing the treads creak under his weight. He didn't hesitate but entered the dining room without stopping. Patch was still drowsing in one corner.

'Night, Naomi, chile,' he mumbled.

Condon didn't dare reply lest his voice give him away. He breathed easier when he reached the hall. There was no light from under the library door, and he surmised everybody was asleep. He let himself out without a sound, crossed the porch and started toward Emma's house. Before he was clear of the porch, a man emerged from the shrubbery and stepped in front of him. Then the man stepped aside and doffed his hat.

'Sorry, ma'am, I didn't know who you was. Late, ain't you?'

Condon tensed. To reply would be to give himself away and not to reply would arouse suspicion. He hesitated too long.

'Hey, wait a minute,' the man growled. 'You mighty tall for a gal.'

Condon's hand tightened on the gun, hidden in the folds of the skirt. The man still had his hat off, and he stooped down to peer at Condon's boots, lifting the hem of the skirt as he did so. With one swift movement,

Condon brought the gun down behind the man's ear and felt him crumple against his legs. Danger became a living thing, and Condon moved instinctively. He rolled the man's unconscious form into the shadow of the shrubs and, picking up the skirt, ran for Emma's with the last dregs of his strength.

At the shed, Condon tore the skirt off, mounted stiffly to the saddle, and headed south without a backward glance.

CHAPTER FIVE

In the grove of junipers a mile south of the house, Condon waited impatiently.

Naomi came so quietly he was unaware of her presence until she was upon him. She had learned well from the Indians at the Mission school.

'How did you get away?' he asked.

'Never mind,' she said, sitting her Indian pony as though she and the pony were one entity. 'Mount up and follow me.'

The urgency in her voice silenced him, and, dragging his weary body once more into the saddle, he followed her at a fast canter. He was past feeling the pain of his shoulder, and the jogging of the horse bacame a rhythm to put him to sleep. He fought to keep awake as they traveled south mile after mile. Then he knew they were in the foothills, going up the breast of the mountain.

There was still a glimmer of moonlight from the crescent moon, and Condon saw a forest of tall pines around them. This continued for some distance, and then he was riding through a narrow opening that brushed his legs on either side of the saddle. The narrow opening finally widened, and they were in a small basin, the size of which could not be estimated in the thin light. In a natural cave-like shelter beside a spring, they stopped.

'Now you can sleep, and sleep good,' she said in a low voice. 'I've got another job to do.'

He managed to get his saddle off and drop it on the bed of rushes that was in the shelter. He pillowed his head on the saddle, and was asleep before Naomi was through covering him with the saddle blanket.

When he finally awoke, the sun was high in the sky. He lay for a moment, confused and mystified by his surroundings, and then the happenings of the night before came back to him. He rose, feeling immensely refreshed; even the pain of his wound had become a dull ache. He doused his head in the cold water of the spring and drank deeply. Then he stood and surveyed his surroundings in wonder.

The shelter was not a real cave; it was just a crude sort of lean-to where two giant boulders had come together. Brush almost hid the opening to the natural room, and brush concealed the back opening completely. The basin itself was a little more than a green hollow in the hills, scooped out by some fluke of nature. There was water and there was grass. The horse he had ridden was grazing nearby. Inside the shelter was food, left by Naomi, and he pounced upon it, eating hungrily.

His hunger sated, he felt as though he had been reborn. What an Eden to rest and grow strong in. It was too much to hope that this hideaway was unknown except to the girl, but if it could escape the search he was sure was being made for him, at least for a week or ten days, then he could fight his battles alone. He flexed his right arm several times, and though the soreness was still there, each attempt made the effort easier. His gunbelt and gun were lying by the saddle, and after buckling them on, he felt once more a complete man. However, his draw was pitifully inadequate. The balance of the day he spent resting, exercising, and eating, regaining his strength to such an extent the nightmare of the past days seemed like a distant memory.

Naomi came at night when he was asleep, and when he awakened he realized how vulnerable he was to capture. The moon had fattened somewhat, and he could see her face, a white blur framed by her dark hair.

'I couldn't come in the daylight,' she explained; 'they were watching me. I brought your rifle and boot.'

'What happened?'

'They found the man you slugged.'

'Was he dead?'

'He didn't come to for a couple of hours, but he'll live.'

'Do they know the part you played in my escape?'

'Nothing for sure.'

'What about Patch?'

'He said he didn't see anybody.'

'But he did.'

'Look, Carl . . .'

'You might as well know my real name,' he interrupted her, 'I'm Cliff Condon.'

'Maybe you shouldn't have told me. I could lie easier the other way. But about Patch: he's Vern Gregory's man. He wouldn't go against Vern, but sometimes where Emma and I are concerned, he isn't *for* Vern. I didn't get to bed until just before daylight.'

'What were you doing?'

'I had to make a false trail for the dogs to follow.'

'Dogs?'

'Vern Gregory's dogs, like the one who guarded you out in the brush. He has a pack of them, and keeps them in the line shack in the back country. Sometimes he gets Patch to rub a powder in their fur that makes them glow at night like ghosts. At first he used them to scare off the Apaches—they never raid our herds any more.'

'Who takes care of the dogs?'

'Cal Moses, an old recluse who pretends to be prospecting. Vern lets him use the line shack and furnishes him with grub for taking care of the dogs.'

'Are they vicious?'

'To strangers they are. Vern uses them to track down men who try to leave the Massacre without permission. I figured he might use them to track you, so I made a false trail. The dogs know me, and I've trained them to follow a certain scent.'

Again Condon wondered at this strange girl who was so closely attuned to nature.

'I heard no dogs.' He realized he had been sleeping the sleep of the dead.

'He didn't take them out last night; it was too late when they discovered the unconscious guard. He's not using the dogs today. He figures you headed for Hanker, where you could get help. He doesn't know about this place, or my hold on his dogs.'

'Where did you learn these things, Naomi?'

'From the Indians at the Mission school. I brought some of them home with me once, on a holiday, and they showed me this hiding place.'

'Suppose you're followed?'

'I'm careful.'

61

'If I can stay here for a few days and get well and strong again, you won't have to worry about me any more.'

'I'll have to worry about you until I get you off Massacre.'

Condon was silent for a moment; then he said gravely, 'I can't leave the Massacre, Naomi. I've a job to do here, two jobs. Gregory is bragging about something big coming up, and I've got to know where it is. I followed the tracks of five hundred stolen cattle to the Arroyo Diablo, and then they vanished into thin air. My brother is missing along with the cattle, and my best friend was shot by the rustlers and died slowly. If I go away now, I would never come back and pick up the trail again.'

'Gregory told you about his plans,' she said quickly, 'because he was testing you. If you were Carl Gabler, he had nothing to worry about. But if you were a stranger—a lawman and bounty hunter to boot—he could never let you leave the Massacre alive. He wouldn't have to murder you himself. He could turn the wolf dogs on you, and they would tear you to pieces.'

*   *   *

Emma Beyer, slouch hat pulled down over her straight black hair, held the reins slack, letting the team of bays pick their way down the tortuous road leading off the mesa to the river. Behind her, perched high on the freight wagon, Gust Allen swayed with the rumble and rattle of the wheels. The smell of the river came up from the canyon into which they descended.

They reached the river, and luckily the raft that served as a ferry was on their side. She helped Patch set the planks that spanned the short distance from the shore to the wide raft. When she had led the buckboard team aboard, they moved the planks over and pulled the big freight wagon alongside the buckboard. Then Patch snapped the chain onto the big pulley wheel that rolled on the cable strung diagonally across the stream. Patch poled the raft into the current, the force of which would push the raft across to the other side. There they drove the wagons off, stacked the planks, and tied the raft to a stake driven in the bank, to be ready for the next user.

They headed up the canyon from which poured Ghost Creek, and finally reached the town of Hanker, a dreary collection of shacks and false fronts spread across a wide spot between the cliffs and extending up and down stream. Though they had started from Massacre at daybreak, it was now late afternoon. A few mangy dogs skulked out of their way as they drove through the dust to the barn at the rear of the general store.

There was no livery stable in the camp, so Prentiss kept the barn stocked with horse feed for his out-of-town customers.

'Care for the team, Patch,' Emma said. She fished into the pocket of the pants she wore and handed the Negro a paper. 'That's the list of supplies. Tell Prentiss he won't have to work late loading them; we won't be going home tomorrow.'

'Yes'm, Miz' Emma.'

'I want you to keep an eye out for that man—Carl Gabler.'

'He may be in one of the bars, ma'am.'

'Ain't you never been in a bar, Patch? You're a grown man. Walk in and act like you belong there.'

'You mean I can drink liquah, jest like them other fellahs?'

'You ain't a slave no more, Patch. You're free as anybody. Here's some money. First off, take the supply order to Prentiss, but tell him no hurry. Then you find that man I fixed up, but don't make no trouble with him. You come to me. You know where I'll be.'

The Negro took the money, his eyes big as he stared at it. 'You-all figgah I'll be all right in a bar alone?' he said hesitantly.

'There's enough half-breeds and Indian trash around here so's it won't make you seem too odd, Patch. Just watch the liquor, and take it easy. You've snitched enough of Vern's brandy so your stomach won't be a

64

stranger to it. Smell the rotgut to make sure it ain't doped. You ain't got enough money to take a beating for it.'

'What I'm going to say to this Carl Gabler iffen I find him, ma'am?'

'Just bring him to me, Patch.'

She watched the Negro go eagerly into the big barn of a store. Then she walked stiffly up the back alley toward the two-story rear end of the Gay Lady, one of the two saloons that catered to the flotsam and jetsam that tarried there.

Emma's feet, in the cobbled boots, moved faster as she neared the back stairs. Skirting a pile of rubbish and two empty barrels, she climbed the weathered stairs to the small porch above. She opened the door without hesitation; it was never locked. Though the outside of the Gay Lady was a box of weathered boards with pine strips covering the cracks, the inside of the apartment into which she stepped was intensely feminine.

The whole posture of Emma Beyer's body changed as she closed the door, sagging a little, making the rough clothes she wore look loose and empty. A strange expression softened her face, and she was like a harried animal that had found sanctuary. Her eyes looked almost with reverence at the fancy room, the lace curtains at the windows, a satin spread on the bed, the carpet on the floor and wallpaper gay with flowers. There were two soft chairs, and a china lamp with a painted shade on the small table.

Before she had her stiff denim jacket off, there was a knock on the door, and it opened without her bidding. Vinnie Goode, who ran the Gay Lady, walked in, big and bold, her brassy hair in ringlets around her square, strong-boned face. Her blue eyes lit up at the sight of Emma, and her painted lips smiled a welcome. She had a bottle of whiskey in one hand, with a glass inverted on top of it. From the pocket of her dress she drew another glass.

'I'll have the first one with you,' she said.

Emma was already pulling the cork from the bottle with her teeth, her hand shaking as she poured the amber fluid into the glasses.

'I've been saving this bottle of good stuff for you, Em. It came in with the last shipment of rotgut.'

Emma took a long drink, felt the liquor burn her stomach, travel through her veins, and smooth out the wrinkles in her nerves. She heaved a long sigh.

'Thanks, Vin—thanks for keeping this hideaway room for me. Sometimes I've just got to let go.'

'I heard the freight wagon coming up the road,' Vinnie said. 'I been expecting you'd be in for supplies about now. Got some bath water heating in the kitchen. Let me help you out of those hideous boots and pants. You can't make yourself a man by wearing a man's clothes, Em. You're too much of a woman for that.'

'Once I was,' Emma said dully as Vinnie knelt and pulled off her boots.

'You could be again if you gave up your crazy ideas. Charley Beyer didn't ask you to take his place.'

'He didn't ask me. A person has to have a dream to live by, and I have mine. I've just about got it made, if only there ain't no hitch. Did the mail come in?'

'The weekly stage is late; should be in tomorrow,' Vinnie said, jerking off Emma's stiff pants with an expression of disgust.

'Did you see a strange cowboy in town today, Vin? His right arm is sore, and he's got a head of unruly brown hair. His face is rough for his age, but his eyes are honest.'

'Has he got a name?'

'Calls hisself Carl Gabler, but that ain't it.'

'What's the problem? You got all kinds of rustlers and gunnies on the Massacre.'

'I gotta stop trouble, Vin, before it starts. And I want to stop it without having him killed,' Emma said doggedly.

'I didn't see him,' Vinnie assured her. 'Now get in the kitchen and scrub that ranch smell off. I'll bring your things.'

Emma took another drink right from the bottle, and her glow of well-being increased, unlocking her mind from its prison of worry

67

and despair. She went into the adjoining room, which Vinnie used as a kitchen and which separated Vinnie's living quarters from this back bedroom. Vinnie had already poured the water into the wooden tub, and Emma climbed in with a contented sigh.

Vinnie came back carrying a silk nightgown and a kimono trimmed with lace. She carried pink bedroom slippers with pompons. Without comment she scrubbed Emma's back as they exchanged gossip about the town. When Emma was toweled and dressed, Vin looked at her with approval.

'You're a caterpillar turned into a butterfly,' she said. 'You're still a handsome woman, Em, if you'd only let yourself be one. Why you slave and fuss over that spoiled brat of Vern Gregory's, I'll never know. Your own kid's got more guts and gumption and common sense. Of course Maxine's beautiful, she's educated, she's talented, but all that came easy to her. Naomi is like you, ignoring the real beauty she has, the soft eyes, the strong face, the raven hair. If you didn't try to take after the Indians, you could rival that beauty of Maxine's.'

'I don't want to rival the beauty of Maxine. Let's drop the subject.'

'Get back to your bottle,' Vin shrugged. 'I'll bring you some food later.'

*   *   *

Vinnie came in with breakfast on a tray before Emma could get from under the covers Vinnie had thrown over her the night before.

'You're going to be a lady while you're here,' Vinnie said with her throaty laugh.

'Did you see Carl Gabler last night?' Emma asked without preliminaries.

'Eat first; then I've got something to tell you. When I brought your supper last night, you were sawing wood a cord a minute.'

Emma, her healthy appetite taking over, devoured the ham and eggs, the hot cakes and the pot of coffee.

'You've got the appetite of a farm hand at threshing time.' Vinnie smiled. 'Wish I could eat like that.'

'What you got to tell me?' Emma asked, wiping her mouth with the napkin.

'That darky of yours almost reopened the Civil War right here in Hanker. He kept dogging everybody in town about the guy Gabler, wanting to know if they'd seen him or knew him. He kept making trips between the Gay Lady and Jose's Iron Bucket across the street, drinking in each place like a good customer ought, but not burning up the rotgut as fast as he was stocking it in. You know how evenings are. Common sense gives way to whiskey talk. The men decided Patch was a spy for the law, and that was why he was asking so many questions. They decided

69

to make him talk about it, but before the conversation was over three men were lying on the floor with knots on their heads, two others were draped over the card tables, and the others were hollering for a lynch rope. I chased them all out and hid Patch in the liquor cellar, locking him in. Never saw such a sight. He was bellowing like a black giant, his shirt tore off and blood on his face. I hope he didn't bust in a whiskey barrel and help himself; he'd tear down the town with his bare hands.'

'Is he all right?'

'I haven't had the nerve to look. Sounds like he's sleeping off the rotgut; one thing that stuff does is make you sleep sound.'

'Is the mail in?'

'Badger Joe, a trapper, just rode in and says he helped Reagan, the driver, get a wheel back on up the canyon. They'll be in soon. You're not rushing off, are you?'

'I figured to spend a day, but if Carl Gabler ain't in town, I got to get back to the ranch. He could be in bad trouble.'

'Trouble's no stranger around here, Emma.'

'This is different. I got a feeling that he might be the man for Naomi. Just my idea; don't spread it around.'

Dressed in her pants and boots, Emma walked back to the store and found her wagon already pulled inside and just about loaded.

70

Surprised, she caught Prentiss and his helper Jed putting the last of the sacks of flour aboard. The store, a big barnlike structure, had a roadway down the middle so that wagons could be driven inside and purchases loaded on directly from the counters. The only post in that forsaken land, it carried everything from pots and pans to harnesses and saddles.

'How come you got my load on, Prentiss?' she asked, mystified.

'After that ruckus last night, I figured you'd be pulling out. Me and Jed got here in the dark and started loading.'

'The mail in?'

Her question was answered by the stamping of hooves and the rattle of wheels as the stage pulled up in front of the store. The driver, a tall, gaunt man with a drooping mustache, beat the dust off his body as he stormed into the store. He was cursing the road, the weather, the horses, and the coach.

'So help me Gawd, I ain't herdin' no more of these consarned contraptions, not over this road. Got held back in Tooker by a gent who insisted he had a wire comin' in he had to get off on the stage. There weren't no wire at all; just the mail bag. I had to knock the galoot down to get on the road. But the buzzard had jimmied one of the wheel bolts, and halfway here I lost a wheel. Danged if he didn't come out of the brush with a gun and try to steal

71

the mail bag. Badger Joe showed up and drove him off with his rifle; nicked him, I think. He didn't get the mail bag, anyways. Must of been something in there he wanted right bad.'

'What did he look like? Did you know him?' Prentiss asked.

'He had bushy brown hair and eyes that looked right through you,' the driver said.

Emma tensed as she listened. Could Gabler have reached Tooker, hoping to intercept the letter from Kile? A crowd was gathering outside, as the coming of the stage was a weekly event, and the mail was the one bright spot in their hard, humdrum lives. Prentiss opened the mail bag, dumped the letters on the counter and called out names. There were three letters for the Massacre: one to Maxine from a friend in Denver; one, which smelled faintly of perfume, for Mex Embozo; and one to Vern Gregory with a Mescosa postmark. This last Emma put inside her shirt when nobody was watching; the other two she slipped into the wide band of her haggard sombrero.

She found Patch at the wagon, a woebegone expression on his face. He looked at her with bloodshot eyes.

'Ma'am,' he said, 'I didn't find Gabler. Let's not talk about the rest of it, huh, Ah'm ready to leave this town right now. Another day wouldn't do me no good!'

CHAPTER SIX

On the third day after her last visit, Naomi came in broad daylight, shortly after noon. She brought another store of food. Cliff was startled at how relieved and pleased he was to see her.

'I almost gave you up,' he said, taking her hand.

She didn't draw her hand away, although her fingers stiffened at his touch. 'I couldn't chance coming here,' she said, her brown eyes soft. 'They watched me all the time.'

'But you're here now—in the daylight,' he protested.

'Mother went to town for supplies the day after you escaped. She insists on going for some reason she keeps to herself. She picked up the mail. She got home yesterday.'

'Was there a letter from Kile?'

'Not that I know of. She said she learned in Hanker that you had gone through there. You were seen in Tooker by the stagedriver; you made the stage lay over while you waited for a wire; and when the win didn't come you tried to rob the mail but were chased off.'

'What made her think it was me?'

'The description: bushy brown hair and deep eyes. If she made it up, she was very convincing, and Gregory swallowed the story.

They quit looking for you on the Massacre. He sent Max Embozo to trail you to Tooker, so today I was free to ride where I pleased. It pleased me to ride here.' She flushed a little at the admission.

'It pleased me have you ride here,' Condon assured her. 'Some day I'll show you how big my pleasure is. Right now I need my horse, Bolo. Have you seen him?'

'He's gone.'

'Gone? If Longest marked him—'

'Ace had nothing to do with it. He was fixing to brand him with a mark the size of Texas. I slipped out in the night and turned him loose. I whipped him and beat him and drove him into the Goosenecks to join the wild ones.'

'But why?' he asked sharply. 'I need him. It will take me days to catch him now.'

She looked steadily at him, her face upturned. 'You have a horse to ride away on.'

'But I can't ride away now.'

'Whether you accomplish your purpose or not, you'll ride away, Cliff. As long as your horse is here, I know you'll come back.' There was a catch in her voice.

Condon took a deep breath, and his arm drew her close to him.

'No matter what happens, Naomi, I will never forget you,' he said quietly.

'I have dreams enough,' she told him stiffly. 'I have memories, Cliff. What I need is

74

substance. I need you . . .'

Cliff put a finger on her lips. 'Not yet, Naomi. My mother had a saying that goes: What *must* be *will* be, but all in good time. Right now I've got a job to do, and further complications can only increase the difficulty and intensify the danger.'

'But why must you stay? Let Vern Gregory ply his crooked trade. Forget the men as though I had burned them with the posters you carried. Of what good are cattle when you are dead, and why must you kill or capture men whose destiny is written on a bullet?'

'No man is alone, Naomi. His bones and his flesh are material of which he makes use, but they are not the man. The man is an invisible spirit of thought, emotion, courage and loyalty. In these things he is connected to all other men by a web as subtle as sunlight, but stronger than steel. A friend is dead and his killer is unpunished; thievery is a blight that destroys both the thief and the victim. These are things that good men know and bad men forget, and the bad men must be made to remember, lest all men forget.'

Her eyes were misted with tears, but her mouth was firm. 'Sometimes goodness is as hard to understand as evil,' she said softly. 'I'll help you find your horse.'

★   ★   ★

They rounded a low butte and entered a grove of junipers so profuse as to be almost impenetrable. Naomi held up her hand and stopped her pony.

'Leave our horses here,' she said, and dismounted.

Condon drew his rifle from the boot as he levered himself to the ground. He followed her through the tangle of trees until, coming to the edge of the grove, she motioned him to stop. She lay on her stomach, Indian fashion, and Condon stretched out beside her. His eyes swept the scene below them, and a strange drama unfolded as they watched.

He saw a herd of wild horses in a meadow between the trees and the tall red columns. The mares and colts were grazing apprehensively, while their buckskin stallion snorted and pranced about them, his head thrown up defiantly, and Condon knew at once it was Bolo! A deliberate but deadly duel was shaping up in the meadow, between the two magnificent stallions, for possession of the mares.

The buckskin had possession of the herd, and he meant to keep it as long as he had the courage and the strength. He wheeled and trumpeted before the intruder who threatened his supremacy.

Bolo, wheeling in close, trumpeted his challenge, and then, by a sudden reverse maneuver, attempted to get between the buckskin and the mares and drive the mares to do his bidding.

The buckskin was too wise to be fooled and too quick to be avoided. He pivoted on one foot and, lunging like a catapult, he rammed his shoulder against the shoulder of the pinto, throwing him off balance. With a squeal the buckskin reared sharp hooves lashing out at his stumbling opponent. The pinto lurched aside, and the sharp hooves hammered against the ground. While the buckskin stood momentarily stunned by the sudden shock of his own weight against the earth, the pinto plunged in, teeth bared, and fastened himself to the buckskin's throat.

'He's magnificent,' Naomi breathed. 'How did you ever tame him?'

'Patience and kindness. I pity the man who ever puts a whip to him,' Condon said.

'Look—look; the buckskin's shaking free,' she said. 'I caught him once by stalking him for two days—I put my hand on him and gave him a sugar lump.'

'And he got away from you?'

'I didn't try to keep him. I called him Nugget. His neck's going to be torn open,' she said fiercely.

Condon felt a stab of pity. He knew how he loved Bolo, but Bolo had been tamed and useful and would be again.

'I'm sorry,' he said.

'Don't be. Nugget will fight his own battle, win or lose. It's nature's way; the strong survive,' she said bitterly.

Nugget tore loose, but blood was smeared over his golden neck.

'There are different kinds of strength, Naomi,' he said softly. 'There's the strength of body, and there's the strength of spirit. If the spirit is weak, the body is useless.'

The two horses, squealing and trumpeting, were sparring in circles, their hooves pawing the air. The buckskin, frenzied over his torn neck, lashed out in a supreme effort, and Condon, seeing the blood-smeared neck, realized that Bolo could be maimed or crippled. This was a fight to the finish, and only the death of one horse could save the other. He caressed his rifle, his hands eager to bring it to the defense of the pinto that had served him so well. But to kill the buckskin would be to kill part of the girl beside him, the girl who had saved his life and who was still helping and protecting him.

'God help me,' he said softly, and he didn't know if he were praying for the pinto, for the girl or for himself.

The decision was taken from him as though in answer to his prayer. A horseman rode from behind one of the columns of red earth. It was Ace Longest! Condon felt a chill of hate come over his body. Longest was going to get his way after all. Automatically, he put the rifle to his shoulder, forgetting his wound. Then Naomi's hand was pressing the gun against the ground.

'No—no. If you fire that gun, they will know you are still on the Massacre instead of thinking you are in Tooker.'

Condon realized the wisdom of her advice, but to lie there and see Bolo caught by Ace Longest was more than he could bear. Before any plan of action could be thought of, there was a puff of smoke from Ace's rifle, and seconds later the sound of a shot reached them. The two stallions, shocked out of their private argument, reacted to this new menace. The buckskin wheeled and snorted an order to the mares. Activated by a single impulse, the band set out for the broken country to the west. Bolo snorted defiance, pawed the ground and whirled, heading south among the Goosenecks, and disappearing with Ace Longest at his heels.

Condon jumped up, his face grim. 'I've got to stop him fron catching that horse,' he almost shouted.

'He hasn't caught him yet,' Naomi said calmly. 'That's treacherous country to chase a horse in, what with gullies, bluffs and pinnacles. He won't catch him soon. You circle around to the west and south, and you'll come to Hashknife Wash. It can't be crossed except at two points, and if Ace is going to catch your horse it will be there,

79

unless your horse can jump a span of fifty feet.'

'No horse can jump such a span. What about you?'

'I'll circle around the other way, just in case Bolo doesn't head for the Hashknife. There's some broken country, but I know it all. That's where I caught Nugget and let him go again.'

Condon scrambled back to his horse and pivoted himself into the saddle. He shoved the rifle into the boot and took off, hearing Naomi shout after him.

'We'll circle around and meet about five miles south of here!'

Condon headed his horse down off the bluff at a reckless speed, thinking only of Bolo and the man who was after him.

He finally reached the gash in the earth which he knew must be the Hashknife Wash, but he found no sign of horse or rider. He turned south along the edge of the wash, peering into the depths occasionally, fear gripping him. No horse could leap the width of that wash, but that did not mean that no horse would try. Reaching one of the crossings Naomi had told him of, he studied the trail but found no recent hoof marks. Grimly he turned away from the wash to circle around and meet up with Naomi somewhere out in that beautiful and tortured country.

Riding up to the rim of a bluff that overlooked a circular basin of grassland, Cliff was confronted by a panorama of plains and columns and low mountains. He dismounted to give his horse a breather. Far out on the plain he saw a ribbon of dust, which settled to reveal Ace Longest on a tiring horse, trailing Bolo by two hundred yards. They were coming toward him, taking a course that would eventually bring them to the Hashknife, and he considered going back to the wash to intercept them. Before this plan became an actual decision, he saw Ace Longest stop his horse and raise his rifle.

'Oh, no!' he breathed. He saw the puff of smoke, but the sound never reached him, or if it did he was past hearing. Bolo had disappeared into a swale, but he knew by the way Ace spurred his horse forward that the shot had not missed. So abrupt was his movement in turning toward his mount that the horse shied away and flung his head up so that Condon missed the trailing reins. As he made a second lunge for the reins, the horse whirled and trotted out of reach. Condon cursed. He realized by the way the animal kept its feet, that it had used this maneuver before. Condon increased his pace and the horse did likewise, keeping just out of reach. It was a most exasperating dilemma for a rider, especially one in Condon's mood. His rifle, his rope, his canteen were all on the saddle, so he had to think of some subterfuge in order to capture the horse before he was left there afoot without water.

The game of tag went on for a quarter of a mile; then Condon saw a patch of brambles up ahead which promised a solution. Sidling around, he worked his way towards the horse's head and then, waving his hat slowly, turned the animal toward the brambles. As he had hoped, the reigns got tangled on a bush, and before the horse could work them loose, Condon gained possession of them.

Curbing an impulse to rowel and whip the animal, Condon climbed into the saddle and headed as fast as he could to the spot where Ace had done the shooting. Riding around one of the red columns of gravel and earth, he reached a wide swale which was filled with brush and huge boulders. In the bottom of the swale a fire burned, and Ace stood there fanning the flame. In front of Longest lay Bolo, the paint horse, his dignity and courage gone.

A red haze of fury blurred Condon's vision as he rode forward as quietly as he could. Two hundred yards from the fire he dismounted, creeping forward on foot, darting from the cover of one boulder to another. He couldn't shoot Longest without endangering the horse, if the horse was still alive. Through the turmoil of his hate and rage, one spark of reason flickered and stayed his gun. No horse was worth the life of a man, not even Bolo. But there were other ways of getting satisfaction, of giving vent to the fury that whipped and rode him. He was close enough to see that Bolo's feet were trussed securely and that his head was dallied close to a thick brush.

Ace, gloating over his victory and confident of his seclusion, picked the red-tipped running-iron from the blaze with his gloved hand, unmindful of the heat that burned through the leather. He kept wide of the bound hooves of the horse, and approached his hip from the back. So intent was he upon his satanic task he was totally unprepared for the buzz saw that hit him.

Condon struck from the rear, slamming into Ace's back and sending the red hot iron hurtling through the air to come to rest in a clump of brush and start a fire of its own. Ace was flung clear across the horse, into the thrashing hooves that kicked and pummeled him in spite of the ropes that held them. Condon circled, and when Ace rose with a black mask of rage upon his face, he was ready for him. He struck Ace's dazed and foxy face with a jabbing left hand that raked and tore the skin. Then he swung his right, and not until then did he remember his wound. An exquisite fury of pain reminded him of it.

There was no retreat; even if he had to die

there was no retreat.

Trying to favor his wounded side, Condon fought with his left foot forward, jabbing with his left, then countering with his right. But the hours of fever and infection had taken their toll. He was sucking for air, trying to keep out of Ace's reach. Somehow he got a second wind, dredged up strength from somewhere and cut Ace's face. Ace, bellowing under the punishment and unused to fighting without a gun, barged in and, hooking his spur behind Condon's ankle, jerked his feet out from under him. Condon fell on his back, and for one instant he could not move. The wind had been driven from his lungs, and the pain of his shoulder was like a hot iron burning into his flesh. Cursing savagely, Ace Longest barged in, aiming a kick for Condon's shoulder, threatening to stomp and trample him into unconsciousness.

'Hold it right there, Ace!' a cold, even voice threatened. 'Move your foot, and I'll blow your leg off!'

Ace spun around, staring at Naomi as though he were seeing a ghost. 'Why, you crazy filly, you trying to scare *me*?'

'I don't care if you're scared or not. If you want to be dead, try to kick him.'

'You ain't got the guts to shoot that gun.'

The rifle at the girl's hip barked, and a shred of cloth whipped away from Ace's sleeve, leaving a tinge of red. His swarthy skin turned a dead gray color. He picked up his hat from the ground and mounted his horse. By this time Cliff was on his feet. Ace stared at him like an executioner.

'You marked me and bled me. No man can do that to me and live. And you, Naomi, I'll fix you so you'll wish you were dead.'

Silently, Condon and the girl watched him ride away.

'Thanks, Naomi,' Condon said, picking up his hat and dusting himself off. 'I reckon God did make guardian angels. You must be mine.'

'I don't have wings, Cliff. I saw you start after him from the bank of the swale. I left my horse and sneaked up through the boulders. Thank God I was in time.'

'If I hadn't had the wind knocked out of me, I think I could have taken him. My shoulder is sore as the devil, but the wound didn't open.'

'You'll have another chance to take him, and you'd better be ready with your gun. In a way he did you a favor; he caught your horse for you.'

Cliff turned his attention to the trussed animal. 'I thought he was trying to kill him.'

'There's some blood on his mane. Ace must have creased him and knocked him out for a spell.'

'Only a dead shot would take such a chance. A miss of two inches, and you've got a dead horse.'

'He's a beautiful animal,' Naomi said. 'Here's a sugar lump. While you get him on his feet, I'll fetch our horses.'

Condon loosed the rawhide hogging strings from Bolo's feet, talking to him in a soothing voice all the while. He fashioned a hackamore out of the strings, which he put on Bolo's head before he loosened the rope that held his head to the stout bush. The big horse got up with a disdainful grunt, shook himself defiantly and glared around. He made no effort to get away, but took the sugar lump Naomi had supplied and nuzzled Cliff's arm for more. The wild buckskin and his herd of mares were safe. Bolo was back in the man-world again.

Cliff examined the wound on the top edge of the horse's neck, and knew that the temporary paralyzing of the big horse could not have been done more expertly. The scar would be slight, and the mane would cover it. When Naomi returned with the horses, Cliff put saddle and bridle on Bolo and turned the other horse loose.

'He'll drift back to the ranch,' Naomi reassured him as they rode toward the hideout.

CHAPTER SEVEN

Two days later, rested, refreshed, and the hurt of his wound only a dull memory of pain, Condon awoke in the basin and looked about carefully before emerging from the shelter under the rocks. He had tethered Bolo in a thick growth of aspen where he could not be easily seen. The big horse nickered a 'good morning' when Cliff emerged from the shelter to wash his face in the cold water of the spring.

Naomi came back early, arriving while Cliff was still drying his face. Again he marveled how her presence affected him. It made him feel stronger, wiser, a whole man. They had come to understand each other so deeply that few words were necessary to convey their feelings. He could tell that she was afraid and worried, and knowing her fear and worry was for him, he put his arms around her. She moved closer into his embrace and looked up at him, her brown eyes glowing.

'We'd better get out of here,' she said without emotion. Only her trembling revealed the depth of her feeling. 'If Vern hears that you're still on the mesa, he'll have the dogs out.'

'And what about you? You were the one who nicked Ace and drew blood.'

She whistled a thin, high sound scarcely audible to Cliff, and out of the brush near the narrow opening came the big dog who had guarded Cliff when he had lain helpless in the brush. The dog whimpered a greeting and, recognizing Cliff's scent, permitted Cliff to pet him.

'If Ace does anything to me, it will have to be from a distance,' she said.

'Where are we going?' Cliff asked.

'To a place where the dogs won't bother you.'

Cliff knew better than to question her. She had saved him; she had helped him retrieve his horse; he had to trust in her knowledge of the Massacre to protect him. He was a man again, his wound immune to punishment, his strong horse between his legs. He must learn what he had to learn as soon as possible and make his plans.

They rode across the breast of the mountain through the thick stand of white pine. Edging toward the north and east, they threaded their way through the gullies of the foothills, the big dog leading the way. Condon studied the land as they rode, a beautiful, lonesome land jeweled with flowers, mantled with grass and gilded by the sun. At one spot where grass had grown over the ruts of wagons, an odd, foreboding landmark confronted them. There was the skeleton wheels of wagons, the iron rims sloughed from the crumbling felloes. At one side some crude crosses built of shards from the wrecks, tilted by time, their arms askew as though weary with the tragedy they bore.

'So this is the spot of the Indian massacre,' he said, stopping his horse.

Naomi looked at him, puzzled. 'You know about it?'

'Maxine told me.'

'How her father had gone scouting for a trail off the mesa, and how he had come back to find everybody murdered and scalped. Only she had been saved by her mother hiding her in her skirts and lying on her. She was an infant and knows nothing about it, except what Vern Gregory tells her.'

'There were no witnesses?'

'Just her father.'

'And what tribe of Indians killed them?'

'Apache.'

'This isn't Apache country.'

'You said yourself Vern kept the ghost dogs to scare off the Apaches.'

'I have no proof about the massacre, either,' she confessed. 'The Indians at the Mission school have a different story.'

He frowned, wondering what she was getting at.

'What kind of Indians are at the Mission school?'

'Navajo; some Hopis.'

'Then this was Navajo country?'

'It was before the reservation. The Navajos are not bloodthirsty, nor are the Hopis.'

'The Navajos were no angels until Kit Carson subdued them.'

'They were protecting their sheep, which were their life. Carson destroyed their sheep, and made sheep out of them.'

'What's their version of the massacre?'

'The white men were starving. The weaker ones were killed and eaten by the stronger. Then winter and the wolves killed the rest,' she said grimly.

Condon felt a cold shock at the story of starvation and cannibalism. It was beyond belief. Horrible as Maxine's story had been, it was preferable to this. Yet such a thing had happened years before in California.

'Do you believe the Indians?'

'You've met Vern Gregory. Does he impress you as fool enough to get lost? Or as a man brave enough to dare the wilderness single-handed? Or as a man sentimental enough to build a ranch in an isolated country to be near the grave of his wife?'

'He could be all of those things. I know little about him. He runs a tough outfit here,' Condon said, wondering.

'He gives the orders.'

'What does your mother, Emma, say about the massacre?'

'Nothing. Believe what you want, but we'd better ride on.'

As they rode from the ominous spot, Condon's mind groped into fearful places. Could Gregory have been one of the cannibals? Could he have survived, with his baby, Maxine, by eating the flesh of the others? This was impossible to believe. The Indians had made up a story to absolve themselves of the crime.

When they neared the Huckleberry line shack, she bade him remain concealed in a grove of juniper while she went on ahead with the big dog.

When she signaled him to advance, he rode into the high-fenced stockade while she closed the gate behind him. There was a fair-sized log cabin in the centre of the stockade, and in one corner a horse shelter with a shed for saddles and grain stood against the stockade fence. From the gloomy interior of the cabin stared a pair of shiny eyes, unblinking and immovable. A half-dozen wolf dogs roamed the stockade, apparently under the spell of Naomi, who walked among them, crooning and stroking.

'How have you tamed them like this?' he asked, a curious tingle going up his spine as the dogs prowled about him.

'Kindness and bribery,' she said, doling out sugar lumps. 'Come; touch them so they can get used to you. It might mean your life; they could tear a stranger to pieces in no time at all.'

Stemming a feeling of panic, Condon put his hand on the shaggy heads and scratched the pointed ears. As the dogs prowled in the dark shadow of the walls, the phosphorescence could be noticed in their fur. He could well imagine the Indians avoiding the Massacre with the ghost wolves prowling the range.

'Why doesn't he keep the dogs at the ranch house?' Condon asked.

'Because they would be howling at every disturbance, every coming and going of the men. Either that, or everybody might make friends with them and destroy their usefulness. Here he keeps them hungry and isolated.'

'How does he manage them?'

'He feeds them extra meat when he comes here, feeds them by hand strips of dried venison and beef. He also uses a whip. The dogs obey him through a strange mixture of need and fear. Let them get your scent, so if he sets them after you, you may have a chance to avoid being torn to pieces, I brought you here to live because it's the most unlikely place for him to search for you. If he takes the dogs out, it will be on a wild goose chase. You can sleep in the shed by the stable.'

'But my horse, Bolo? I can't hide him here.'

'Cal Moses will take care of him. Come on and meet him.'

The interior of the cabin was almost dark, for the only light came through the door. There was a window with a wooden shutter, but the shutter was closed. Condon stared at the man with the shiny, immovable eyes. He saw a figure dressed in worn buckshin, with shaggy hair streaked with gray falling to his shoulders, and shiny eyes like pieces of glass behind bushy brows. The nose was patriarchal; the mouth was hidden in a mass of tangled hair. The eyes held Condon's interest, for behind that glassy surface he recognized pain, the agony of a soul condemned without hope.

'Cal, this is Cliff Condon,' Naomi said.

The hand that extended from the frayed buckskin sleeve was calloused and as gnarled as the knot of an oak. Condon winced at the leathery feel of the skin as he took the hand, but was amazed at the strength of it.

'How.' The Indian greeting had the grating quality of a voice unused to talking. Moses uttered another single word, 'Set.'

His eyes accustoming themselves to the dim light in the cabin, Cliff saw a room scrubbed so clean it was as though the owner had tried to remove a stain. There was a bench, a table, a tier of bunks, a fireplace with the ashes brushed neatly off the hearth, with a cast-iron pot hanging from a pothook. In one corner was a ladder leading up to a hole in the loft from which came the odor of jerky.

'Cliff's going to sleep in the shed at the stable. I want nobody to know he's here, understand?'

The eyes shifted under the bushy brows. 'Reckon,' was the laconic response.

'Will you hide his horse and fetch it when he needs it?'

'Reckon.'

'Thank you, Cal. I'll make it up to you somehow.'

'Pray for me.'

There was such a deep note of hopeless pleading in the words, it stirred Condon strangely. Outside, he asked, 'Can you trust him?'

'I do. I'd trust him with my life.'

'How come? He's a strange hombre.'

'Because I feel in my heart he's honest. Men are twisted in strange ways by necessity and tragedy, but a truly honest man is always honest. He is suffering, and there must be a reason for it, a reason that still festers in him. Because I ask it, he won't betray you.'

'Another thing,' Cliff said, a little disturbed by his situation. 'If there was no letter from Kile, if Emma says I was seen in Tooker, why must I hide from Gregory?'

'There *was* a letter,' Naomi said, her brown eyes looking at him frankly. 'I found it in Emma's room. It had been opened, and she had not given it to Gregory. It said Gabler

94

was coming, all right, but he won't be here for two more days. Mex Embozo came back to the ranch with the man who had been seen in Tooker. He was one of our men. He looks a lot like you. What wire he was looking for or why he wanted to rifle the mail sack, I don't know.'

Condon stood for a moment digesting all this, and a slow rage fermented in him.

'Why did you wait until now to tell me all this?' he demanded.

'Because I know you, Cliff. You would have taken off in spite of me, without me, and you would have tried to find your cattle and your men in a big rush. Do you know the danger you're in?'

'How can I avoid danger?'

'By going slow, by staying here, by getting help if you can. You've got two weeks. The barges won't be on the river for two more weeks. It says so in the letter. Here you're safe from Gregory, and you're safe from the dogs. Have you ever seen a man mangled by wolves? Well, I have!'

With that she led her pony outside the gate, the big dog following meekly at her heels. Closing the gate, she mounted and rode away without looking back.

When Naomi had gone, Condon stood in the door of the line shack with a queer, eerie feeling at being confined in the weird place. Regardless of what Naomi thought, it was more of a trap than a sanctuary.

Without turning his head, he said to Moses, who was behind him in the cabin, 'I can't stay here, you know. She's done too much for me already. Because of me, she's in bad danger from Ace Longest, and she'll get herself into worse trouble. I've got to keep away from her and do what I came here to do.'

'Yup,' the old man agreed.

'I'll take my horse and go.'

'Nope. After dark.'

'I don't know the country well enough to travel at night.'

'I do. Feed the dogs, make friends with them. Meat's in the loft.'

The cryptic words of Cal Moses left no room for argument. He did not even ask what Cliff meant to do on the Massacre. Because making friends with the wolf dogs seemed so important to Naomi and to Moses, Cliff climbed the ladder to the attic and brought down the strips of jerky. It was mostly venison, good enough to stay the hunger of man. When he went into the yard, the dogs swarmed about him, sending up a weird chorus that chilled the blood. He doled out the meat, giving each dog a generous portion.

Washing his hands in a water trough near the stable, Cliff went back to the cabin to find Moses busy.

'I'd better go,' he said again, not knowing

how much he could trust the trapper.

'Eat first,' Moses said in his rusty voice.

Moses had poked up the fire under the iron kettle, and there was a coffeepot setting in the coals. On closer inspection, Condon noticed how meticulously neat and clean the room was. Even the tin cups shone as though polished. Cal Moses went to a bench in one corner and, dippering water from a bucket into a tin basin, washed his hands over and over. He was like a huge figure out of the Bible, or Pilate washing his hands to absolve himself.

Drying his hands, Moses took the sourdough crock from the shelf above the fireplace. Pouring the bubbling ferment into a hollow of flour he made on a mixing board, he stirred flour into the thin batter until it was of a consistency to make a loaf. This he baked over the fire in a clay vessel which served as an oven. Hanging from a pothook was another pot in which turnips and meat simmered.

Range riders seldom got fresh vegetables, and when Moses saw Cliff staring at the turnips, he volunteered:

'I've got a garden outside the stockade.'

Condon didn't realize how hungry he was until he sat down. The meal consisted of beans, turnips cooked with jerky, and sourdough bread. Nothing fancy, but nourishing and filling. He noticed that Moses carefully avoided the meat, eating only the beans and the turnips with bread. When Condon offered him the meat, he refused it.

'I eat only vegetation.'

Condon had heard of people called vegetarians, but he had never met one. In the West, meat was the basic food because it could be found in the most remote places, but vegetables were hard to find. By the time the tin plates had been washed, it was dusk. Moses filled a jar with beans, which he put on the table with what was left of the bread. He brought some of the best jerky from the loft.

'Take these with you,' he said gruffly.

'I have food in my saddle bags; Naomi brought it to me.'

'You'll need this, too. If you were wise, you would leave this place, but youth is never wise. There's little chance you'll succeed in your quest. There's a good chance you will die.'

Cliff took his horse from the stable, where Bolo had gotten into the grain bin. Cliff frowned at this.

'You stupid animal,' Cliff scolded him. 'You're not used to heavy feed, and here you go gorging yourself. You'll be lucky if you don't founder. Just for that you don't get much water.'

With Moses leading the way on foot, they left the stockade. It was almost dark, but a quarter-moon yielded a grudging light. The hulking figure of Moses moved ahead with a long, tireless tread, following trails that would have been impossible for the uninitiated.

CHAPTER EIGHT

Hoping to avoid detection, Naomi took a roundabout trail back to her home. She had the big dog with her.

The sun seemed to be setting with alarming swiftness when she emerged from a copse of piñon and looked down into a swale where the Massacre crew were working a herd of cattle. There were eight men working for the Massacre, and four of them were below her. The balance of the crew must be off on a raid, she thought bitterly. She was not sure just how Gregory worked the ranch, but he tried to keep his hands clean, at least in theory. He bought the stolen cattle from the men after they rustled them, for a few cents on the dollar, and had them sign bills of sale. Then he branded them with his tomahawk which could cover anything. What his present scheme was she could only guess. He was about to make a killing, that much she knew, and nothing was going to stand in his way.

She had come out on the ridge so suddenly that she did not realize she was visible to the men below. Even as she hesitated, she saw one of them cut out of the cloud and ride toward the ridge. There was no mistaking the man; he was Ace Longest. Sudden fear goaded her into action. This was her first meeting with Ace since the incident in the Goosenecks, and she had inadvertently given him the advantage he needed. She was halfway between the Huckle Creek line shack and home. She could ride down to the herd, and seek safety in the presence of the other men, but she couldn't stay with them all night. Her only recourse lay in flight.

Her horse had been ridden most of the day and he was tiring, but he responded to her heels. He was a tough, whang-leather cow pony, with the stamina gained from cutting cattle all day. She turned him away from the ridge and headed for home. The big dog, incited by her sudden movement, raced on ahead. She had a start on Ace, and could beat him back to the big house and the corrals. She felt the pony surging between her legs with long leaps, his head out-thrust and his nostrils distended. He couldn't continue the dead run for long, but she had to put distance between herself and the man who pursued her.

She came off the ridge into an open stretch which was dotted with the mounds of ground squirrels, and she shuddered to think what might happen should her horse step into a hole. She dared to look around, and found no

100

one behind her. Breathing easier, she slowed her mount, and spoke soothing words of thanks to him for his efforts. Cantering along, her eyes searched for a sight of the big house and the cottonwoods. She rode close to the foot of the ridge, so in case Ace appeared behind her, she could climb back to the shelter of the trees.

She caught her first glimpse of the big house when Ace rode off the ridge just ahead of her, his swarthy face twisted by a cold smile. Naomi knew that she was trapped. She resisted an impulse to turn and ride back the other way. With a desperate effort, she goaded her pony forward and shouted to the dog. Ace still had in his hand the lasso he had been using on the cattle, the loop ready for throwing. Naomi stiffened, waiting for the loop to hiss toward her. She had to avoid it, but to run ahead of Ace would give him just the chance he needed. No cowboy worth his salt would miss roping a critter running ahead of him, no matter how the animal—or person—dodged.

'Get him, Devil!' she screamed.

Before the big dog could launch himself, Ace's rope hissed out, but not at her; it struck like a snake and tightened about the throat of the dog. The animal was spun halfway through his leap and slammed to the ground, giving him no chance to get his wind. Before the dog could recover from the rope, Ace had him dragged close and dallied to his pommel, with his front quarters off the round. The dog was helpless. He was choking to death. He was making horrible sounds and thrashing about helplessly.

'Let him go, you beast!' Naomi cried. Evil delight was a living thing in Ace's face.

'You marked me, girl, and made me crawl. Did you think that was the end of it?'

'I had to do what I did, or you would have killed Condon.'

'Why not? He jumped me.'

'Because you were marking his horse.'

'My horse. I caught him—there was no mark on him. There ain't no law against branding a slick.'

There was truth in what Ace said, but it was only a legal truth with no morality in it.

'You knew it was his horse. He could have killed you—shot you down without warning like you did him. But there's a difference between you and him, the difference between a man and a dog.'

'Are you trying to win my friendship? I *could* break your dog's neck right now. Any more of your compliments, and I will!' Ace said furiously

Naomi realized she could get nowhere by goading him, and hated herself for doing it, but her hatred for him was greater than her fear. She had inadvertently walked into danger, and Ace was forcing his advantage to

102

the horrible limit.

Then, when the dog was ceasing his struggles, a shot rang out from the left of Ace, and the rope that held the dog was severed two inches from Ace's hand. The big dog dropped to the earth like a sack of grain.

'*Señor*, I like not your kind of pleasure,' the smooth voice of Mex Embozo said. And in her stunned confusion Naomi saw the debonair Mexican mounted upon his golden horse, the silver trappings dull with dust, blowing the smoke from the barrel of his gun. 'I, too, saw the girl, *compadre*. Have you nothing better to do than frighten women and dogs?'

The look of savage joy was wiped from Ace's face as he turned toward the intruder. He moved his hands very carefully, away from the gun. If he was not a frightened man, he was a very wary one.

'I have no quarrel with you, Embozo,' Ace said.

'Unfortunately, *amigo*, I have a quarrel with you,' Mex Embozo said quietly. 'I place this *señorita* under the protection of my saint. You will do well to see that no evil befalls her.'

'You got no call to ride herd on me!' Ace said defiantly.

'I waste not the words,' Embozo said. 'I have spoken.'

The dog, rousing from his stupor, was

103

struggling to his feet. Ace spun his horse around, turned his back on Embozo and, drawing his gun, shot the dog in the head. Then he dug spurs to his horse.

A wave of nausea sickened Naomi at the sight of the killing. Through tear-stung eyes she saw Mex Embozo deliberately unsheathing his rifle. Desperately she spurred her horse against him and beat the gun down.

'No—no!' she sobbed. 'Don't kill him—not over a dog.'

'But he has hurt you, *señorita*, more deeply than the wound of a bullet.'

'He had a reason,' she confessed.

Embozo looked at her with a puzzled frown. '*Quien sabe?*' He shrugged. '*Adios, señorita.*' Tipping his hat, he rode back toward the herd.

Blinded by tears, Naomi, dismounting, ran to the dog and buried her face in his shaggy fur. He had given his life for her—had pitted his strength and courage against hate and cunning and had died uselessly.

'May God take you,' she whispered, and headed for the ranch.

At the big house, Naomi found Patch on the back porch, nursing a kitten. 'His mothah done run off with some tomcat, I expect. Yowlin' his haid off out here. Ah figgahed a little milk won't hurt him.' Then, suddenly noticing Naomi's distraught face and bloody hands, he put the kitten down by the saucer of milk and put his big hands on her shoulders.

'Chile, you-all been crying. How come you shaking like a leaf?'

'I've had trouble, Patch,' she said, closing her eyes. Incoherently she tried to tell him what had happened.

'Lawsy me, lawsy me, chile, that Ace is a right bad man. Want Ah should kill him, say so,' Patch consoled her.

'Let him be, Patch; he'll get himself killed. I want you to go back and bury the dog—that much we can do for him.'

'Sure, chile, Ah'll take care of that for you.'

'It's almost dark; do you think you can find him.'

'Reckon some of that phosphorous powder is still in his hide. Should lead me to him. You want Ah should haul him heah.'

'No—no. Don't let anybody know what happened. Bury him out there. I've got a reason for that, Patch.'

'Iffen you-all mean that driftin' man who got shot up, Marse Gregory knows he's on the Massacre.'

'How does he know, for sure.'

'Max Embozo came back 'thout him. No sign of him in Tooker or Hanker. Ah got busted up some mahself trying to find him. Marse Gregory opines that this heah man ain't a man to quit easy. Marse Gregory ain't a man to quit easy, neither, chile. He figgahs to kill that man and will have the dogs out aftar him. That man come nosin' around heah at the wrong time—a bad time. Reckon Ah bettah get out and bury that dog.'

Patch faded into the dusk, and as Naomi turned she was startled to find Maxine standing in the kitchen door, the lamp behind her making spun gold of her hair. Her head was held proudly on her long white neck, and there was a tone of command in her voice.

'Come in here, Naomi,' she said.

Naomi hesitated. Exhausted, she was in no mood for an argument with Maxine.

'I've been waiting for you,' Maxine said in a softer tone of voice. 'Please.'

The last word was something Naomi had not expected to hear from Maxine. Puzzled, Naomi stepped into the kitchen. In the light of the lamp, the grief on her face, her disheveled appearance, the blood on her hands painted a picture of dejection and defeat.

'What happened to you, Naomi?' Maxine asked.

'Nothing,' Naomi said. Even now she could not help but compare her drabness to Maxine's bright beauty.

'There's blood on your hands. Did you kill someone?'

'A dog.'

'*You* killed a dog? Do you expect me to believe that?'

'I killed him—it was through me he died.'

'Don't be ridiculous. You couldn't kill anything. Have you seen Ace today?'

'Yes.'

'He came to the house the other day and raised a rumpus with Vern because somebody had turned loose the big painted horse. He accused Vern of wanting it for himself. Vern threw him out of the house, threatened to fire him, but Ace laughed at him. Vern can't fire anybody now; he can't let anything upset his plan. He's got everything figured, down to what he's going to do with the money; down to the death of the man who calls himself Gabler. I don't want that man to die!'

Naomi said bitterly, 'You could do nothing for Cliff Condon—that's his name, Cliff Condon—but make his life miserable. Why don't you take one of your Denver men—one of the rich men out there—for the big gold strike? That's what Vern wants you to do.'

'That's what Vern wants,' Maxine said, her red lips twisted. 'Vern wants me to marry some fat old man with a lot of money. Nobody ever asks what I want.'

'You want anything you can't reach—a reflection in the water, the moon in the sky. And if you got them, what would you do with them, Max?'

'I've never had a chance to find out.'

'Condon has a job to do; then he'll be gone,' Naomi said.

'He's going to die, you know, unless we help him.'

'We?'

'I don't want to see him dead any more than you do. Do you think I have some magic powder to make him love me? Do you have a magic powder to make him love you? No. Let him make up his own mind about that, but let's keep him alive. Where is he?'

Tired and goaded and wanting only to rest, Naomi told the whole story from the time she had turned the stallion loose, to his capture, and Ace Longest's threats. She told how Ace had caught her and roped the dog.

'Mex Embozo saved me,' she finished, tears in her eyes.

Maxine's eyes lit up at the mention of Embozo. 'There's a man,' she said softly, 'a strange man, a Mexican. They talk about hot-blooded Latins, but he has ice in his veins.'

Naomi couldn't help but remark, 'How do you know?'

'Mex Embozo is a fugitive from his own past,' Maxine said softly.

A fugitive? It suddenly dawned on Naomi who the man was on the other poster she had burned. One of the men up for bounty was Ace Longest. The other was Mex Embozo!

Suddenly Naomi was surprised to hear herself confiding things she had kept locked in her mind—confiding to Maxine Gregory!

Even as she talked, she was not sure of what Maxine might do with the information.

'Cliff's a lawman,' Naomi said, 'a bounty hunter. He had wanted posters on Ace Longest and Mex Embozo—dead or alive. I tore them and burned them. I hid his badge; I helped him escape and nursed him until he was well again. I didn't do all that to have him killed.'

'What have you done to guarantee he won't be killed? He can't stay hidden on the Massacre forever. Everything you've done has made his position worse. By hiding him in the brush when you first found him, you nearly let him die. He would have died if I hadn't brought him to Emma. By turning loose his horse, you forced him into a fight with Ace Longest. You can't conceal him for long on the Massacre; Vern will have the dogs out.'

'I can delay him from a showdown until Gregory's business is over,' Naomi said hopefully.

'Embozo and Longest will still be alive. Your man still has a score to settle with them—a personal score. He's not a bounty hunter, Naomi; he's a man with a grievance that must be paid with justice or with blood. Where is he?'

Naomi closed her eyes. Here was a side of Maxine she had never seen before, a softer, giving side.

'He's at the Huckle Creek line shack,'

109

Naomi heard herself saying.

The change that came over Maxine sickened her. The softness that had invaded her beautiful face was wiped away by a hard look of triumph, and her lips tightened over her white, even teeth.

'You little fool! You insufferable fool! What makes you think Cal Moses will keep his mouth shut? That crazy old man! Vern won't have to turn the dogs after Condon; the dogs already have him. They're Vern's dogs, you know. Now I'll have to go up to that cursed cabin and talk to that hateful old man. He makes my skin crawl when I think of him. I only saw him once by accident, when I was out riding, and the way he looked at me terrified me. It was the way a man looks at a horse or a dog, something he owns.'

With that Maxine stormed out of the kitchen, and Naomi stumbled outside.

CHAPTER NINE

Cliff was awakened at dawn by an eerie, gasping sound. He sat up quickly, his hand closing on the gun beside him. He saw nobody but Bolo and, jumping up, ran to the big stallion. Bolo was standing with his head down, his nostrils distended and his stomach swollen. He was gasping for every breath and

110

staggering with the effort. Recognizing the trouble, Condon stroked the suffering animal's neck.

'You loco horse, that's what you get for making a hog of yourself in that grain barrel. You haven't been grained for days, and you've got to take it easy.'

The scolding did nothing to relieve the pressure, and Condon knew the horse might die unless he took drastic action.

Cursing under his breath, he took out his stock knife and opened the longest, pointed blade. 'I'm not going to hurt you, boy. I don't like to chance this, but it's your only hope.'

He lit a match, sterilizing the blade, and, carefully selecting the spot where the stomach came close to the muscle, he plunged the blade all the way in and heard the hiss as the gas rushed out. The horse winced but stood firm, and Condon held the wound open until most of the gas had escaped. He heard the horse breathing great gusts of air, and knew that the danger had passed. But it left him in a bad spot. He couldn't tighten the cinch and ride the horse until the blood had a chance to congeal in the wound.

After eating some jerky and cold beans, he did the only thing he could do, saddled the horse with a loose cinch and set off on foot. He was determined to lose the good people who were trying to help him, put them out of danger and be his own man. He headed east through a thick growth of rabbit sage, whose golden flowers left yellow marks upon his clothing.

He kept up a steady, tiring pace, the big horse following docilely at his heels. He topped a flat hill that was covered with juniper, and here he stopped to rest and eat more cold food. The big horse started nipping at the bunch grass, which was an encouraging sign. Having rested, Condon started out again. On foot, he could take directions he would not have attempted on horseback. Toward evening, he found himself approaching the end of the mesa where he had been shot, but farther to the east. He looked down into a shallow arroyo, the upper end of which was wooded with piñon and juniper.

There was a seep of water where he stopped, enough for a man and a horse, and, hobbling Bolo, he prepared to spend the night. Something strange in the bottom of the arroyo attracted his attention. It looked as if well traveled cattle trails emerged from the trees and converged into a wider single trail that led north. Not daring to make a fire, he munched hard bread, jerky and cold beans uncomplainingly. When he felt safe enough, he could kill some game and roast some meat.

Finished eating, he wandered curiously down toward the trails, hoping to inspect them before it became too dark. Stopping in the protection of a clump of high brush, he studied a pall of smoke rising from the trees. Then he realized the smoke was not smoke at all, but dust—the dust of hundreds of hooves. He could hear cattle bawling. How could cattle reach the mesa from the south wall? He had studied every foot of that wall, and had found only the treacherous trail up which he had climbed the day he had been shot.

He moved closer, creeping from brush to brush to avoid detection. Then a herd of cattle—he estimated four hunded head— came bawling from the trees not two hundred yards from his hiding place. It was too dark to read any brands, but he knew they were stolen cattle. The five hundred head of cows stolen from Delgado must have been brought in the same way. But how?

He saw the sagging shoulders of the point riders and knew they had been travelling a long way. The two drag riders were hurrahing the herd ahead. Condon tried to think of some way he could get near enough to the herd to hear the men's conversation. His rope was back at the camp with his saddle. He had nothing with him but his gun. He climbed out on the edge of a twelve-foot ledge where he could get a better view of the action. At the same time, a small bunch of cattle revolted and turned away from the herd toward him.

'Go get 'em, Tex!' he heard one of the drag

riders shout.

'The buzzards ain't getting away now!' the man called Tex shouted, spinning his cow pony after the deserting strays.

Condon saw a man about his own size, with a flat-crowned hat and a sheepskin coat with the collar turned up against the night chill. A dozen longhorns were heading straight for the ledge on which Condon waited.

The bunch of cattle reached the ledge and were forced to veer off. Tex followed them, and started to pass right below Condon. With total surprise on his side, Condon had the advantage he needed. He dropped from the ledge upon Tex's back, and as he did so, he slammed his gun hard against the back of Tex's ear. The cowboy dropped from the saddle like a pole-axed steer, Condon on top of him. The cow pony stopped as soon as the weight left his saddle and stood ground-dallied by the dropping reins.

Making sure Tex was unconscious, Condon pulled off the man's coat and hat. Taking the lasso from the man's saddle, he trussed him up with his own rope. Then he quickly removed his own coat, spreading it over the unconscious man, and pulled on the sheepskin. He traded his own hat for the one with the flat crown. Neither he nor the man had shaved for days. The masquerade was complete. Mounting the cow pony, he spurred him after the bunch of cattle and turned them back toward the trail. It was some time before he caught up with the main herd. When he did, the other drag rider shouted his praise.

'Good work, Tex! Them cows can buy us more fun in Denver.'

Condon faked a cough and, gasping, replied, 'Be glad when this caper's over and I can wash of this here dust out of my pipes.'

It was dark except for the moon, which was nearing the full when they reached the corrals at the main ranch. Here Cliff got his first close look at the point riders who were worrying the cattle into the chute. One of them seemed somehow familiar.

'Hey, Tex, push up them drags!' the cowboy said.

That was all Condon needed—the voice. It was Arny, his brother! There was no time for conjecture, no time to confirm his belief. The cattle were milling, kicking up a cloud of dust, and all hands were needed to worry them into the corral. Before the last cattle were inside, Condon saw the big form of Colt Denger standing in the dust at his knee.

'You'll have to take the first night watch, Tex. Sorry to push you so hard, but Ace cut out for Hanker. Ain't much I can do about it. Get some chow and a fresh horse. Better take the chow with you and eat on the run. The big herd down in the breaks is getting restless.'

Condon coughed again as though clearing his voice. He had never heard Tex talk and could not take a chance on his voice giving him away. Pretending to be choked up, he said, 'Okay, Colt. I've been eatin' enough dust to start a ranch.'

'Well, it won't be long. We can all wash it away with redeye—barrels of it. Good luck. Get a fresh horse from the remuda.'

With Tex's horse, Tex's hat and Tex's coat up about his ears, he went over to the lighted cook shack.

He knocked on the door of the kitchen before he realized that could be a mistake. Tex would no doubt have walked right in. But he wasn't Tex, and the lamplight might give him away. When the short, fat cook opened the door, Condon forestalled his remarks.

'I'm too grimy to come in,' he said. 'Fix me up a bag of grub to take along. I got some night herdin' to do.'

Grumbling, the fat man went back inside, and Condon waited. Denger and Gregory were standing talking at the corner of the building.

'If Kile can get the barges up here while the river is high, the whole operation might take a week,' Gregory was saying.

'I figure we could swim some of them through the slot,' Denger said.

'It's too long a swim. Drowned cattle aren't

116

worth much,' Gregory replied.

'We might have to take some of them down the hole at the south end, the way we brought them in,' Denger suggested.

'It's getting too late in the year for that, Colt. Not enough water. We've got to chance it by the river. If only Kile would send that letter telling us when he'll be here.'

'It's a funny thing, Mister Gregory,' Colt Denger said, 'but Mex Embozo stopped in Hanker on his trip from Tooker. He said Emma picked up the mail. Had one letter for him, which he got by going to Emma's house.'

Gregory said a little impatiently, 'I know that. Maxine got a letter, too.'

'But there were three letters.'

'What do you mean?'

'Could Emma be keeping the letter from Kile?'

'Why? She's in this as deep as the rest of us—maybe for a different reason, but she's in it.'

'She saved the life of the man who called himself Gabler. There could be something in the letter about him, something she don't want us to see.'

'I'll talk to Emma,' Gregory said.

The cook brought the bag of grub to the door and shoved it at Condon, and, having no more reason for standing there, Condon walked past Denger and Gregory without looking at them. He took the reins of his horse and led him toward the shadows of the barn. Inside the barn, a lantern cast a dim light, revealing a saddle pole with brush and currycomb hanging on nails. Realizing that no cowboy worth his salt would turn a tired horse loose without a rubdown, he led the horse inside, removed the saddle and applied the brush vigorously to the animal's sweat-grimed hide.

'You-all wantin' anotah horse?' the voice of Patch said behind Condon.

Condon swung around, surprised. The big Negro stepped forward and jerked off the flat-crowned hat.

'You-all ain't Mistah Tex. I knowed that the minute I saw you brushing that horse.'

'What do you mean?'

'Tex was teetotally left-handed, an' you-all was using yore right hand. What you-all doing heah?'

'Tex got throwed back up the trail. I took his place.'

'You-all in big trouble, suh.'

'Who's the horse wrangler here?'

'Reckon that's me.'

'Wrangle me a horse and forget you saw me.'

'Ah cain't do that, suh. I'm Mister Gregory's man, and Ah go wheah he goes and does what he does. If he goes back to Virginny, I go to Virginny, or New Orleans

118

or maybe Saint Louis. Ah'd like that, suh, but Ah ain't prone to murder. Miss Maxine says should I see you-all, to bring you up to the house so she can talk to you.'

'But I can't go up there now, Patch.'

'Reckon you can't do nothing else, suh. All Ah got to do is holler, and you're done for,' Patch said grimly.

Condon realized the Negro was right. He had more friends on the Massacre than he had dared hope for in the beginning, and to alienate them now might prove disastrous.

'I'm expected at the herd, Patch. If I don't show up—'

'Ah'll ride night watch for you.'

'I'll need a horse.'

'You-all will be bettah off layin' low heah at the home ranch, suh. Ace Longest caught Naomi ridin' home from the line shack the other day.'

Condon felt fear and anger stiffen his spine. 'What did he do to her?'

'Nothin'. Mex Embozo rode up and stopped him. But Ace killed her dog out of orneriness and then rid off. He figured you must be at the line shack. He'll track you till one of you is daid.'

'I'll still need a horse, even if I see Maxine.'

'Ah'll leave one in the shed back of Emma's cabin.'

When he knocked on the front door of the big house, Maxine came out and led him to the shadows of the back porch before she spoke. He could smell her faint, heady perfume, and her classic features under her crown of golden hair were a grim mask.

'What are you doing in that get-up?' she demanded, indicating the flat-crowned hat and the sheepskin coat. 'I thought you were the man called Tex.'

Condon, hoping to learn more from the girl, told her frankly what had happened.

'You're sure eager to get yourself killed, aren't you?' she said. 'Any one of the men here would kill you if they found you snooping around. They've all got a stake in those cattle, and they mean to collect.'

'One man wouldn't kill me; I know,' Condon said, thinking of Arny.

'Try him and see. Every man who comes here to work has thieved and murdered a dozen times over. Do you think they'd be particular here—on the Massacre?' She moved closer to him. 'I don't want you killed, Cliff Condon.'

'You know my name.'

'Naomi told me; she told me about hiding you at the line shack. If you can stand that old man up there, you've got more courage than I have. He gives me the creeps.'

'I think he's a good man. Peculiar, maybe, but harmless. If you want me to stay alive, maybe you can help me. I've got five hundred head of cattle to take back to Colorado, and two men. Ace Longest is one of them.'

'Ace is hunting for you now. You can't take him back alive. Suppose you can't kill him?'

'Then he'll kill me.'

She moved close against him. Taking his hand, she put it to her face. 'Feel my face, Cliff. If it was light, you could see what Ace did to me. He bruised me and cut me because I refused to let him handle me. He tried to force me to tell him where you were.'

Condon felt a warm flood of sympathy go through him. Must all the good people on the Massacre suffer because of him?

'I'm sorry,' he said contritely, instinctively drawing her into the protection of his arms. Her face was tilted up to him, her moist red lips inviting without brashness. He bent his head and pressed his mouth upon them in a long, lingering kiss that left him with mixed emotions. He had felt restaint in the girl, as though she dared not give too much. He had accepted her lips without reservation, and they had left with a feeling of unfulfillment and doubt. But she didn't draw back, and he continued to hold her.

'Take me away from here, Cliff. Take me away from all the phonies, the thieves, the murderers. I don't need the world. I need a little honesty for a change. You could learn to love me.'

'Loving you would be the easy part,' he said softly. 'You want a man. Until I settle what I came here to do, I'm no man at all—not to myself, who lost a friend to the greed and callousness of men within my reach; not to my neighbors, who trusted me with a job; not to you, who would always suspect a weakness in me; especially not to my brother, who came to the Massacre to throw his life away.'

Maxine drew back sharply. 'Your brother?'

'He's one of Gregory's men now. I don't know what name he goes under.'

'That's your answer? I knew it would be. I can't promise you any help, Cliff Condon. When the showdown comes, I've got to keep a way open for myself.'

'There's a compensation in everything, Maxine. A short vital life might provide more fulfillment than a hundred years of caution,' he said.

'You had better sleep at Emma's. She's on your side,' she said, and went into the house.

Hoping to find Naomi at Emma's cabin, and wanting to tell her how sorry he was about the killing of her dog, Cliff went to Emma's cabin. In answer to his knock, Emma opened the door. At first she didn't recognize him.

'What are you doing here?' she demanded, her comely face worried and perplexed. Her eyes looked tired as though from lack of sleep, and she ran a strong hand through her hacked-off hair.

'I want to see Naomi,' Cliff said, removing his hat.

'So it's you again,' Emma sighed. 'I had hoped to keep you alive, but I reckon there ain't no use in trying to keep a man who's anxious to get killed. But there ain't no sense in you getting Naomi killed, too.'

'That's the last thing I want. I'm sorry about the killing of her dog; I want to tell her that. I didn't ask her to save my life, but if it hadn't been for the two of you I'd be dead. I don't want her to get in any more trouble because of me. I want to tell her that—I want to tell her why I left Cal Moses' shack. What I came here to do, I'll do somehow without her help.'

'She's a growed woman, Gabler.'

'I'm not Gabler; you know that. I'm Cliff Condon from Delgado over in Colorado.'

'Whoever you are, she's in love with you—her first love. Do you think she can stop herself from helping you? As long as you're around here, she'll think of nothing else but helping you. I know. A man puts duty above everything else, even love, but a woman puts a man above duty. I only hope she doesn't get hurt too bad.'

'I don't want to hurt her.'

'Then go away now; forget you ever came here.'

'I can't do that. She understands. Where is she?'

123

'I don't know. She comes and goes as she pleases. She's probably out looking for you. You might as well come in and have some stew. You look dog tired.'

Condon entered the clean kitchen and ate hungrily of the nourishing stew. It was the first hot meal he had had since leaving Cal Moses. When he had finished eating, Emma said, 'There's an extra cot in my room. You might as well stay the night.'

Condon had no intention of sharing her room. 'I'll sleep in the shed at the back. Patch is bringing me a horse. When Naomi comes, tell her where I am.'

Condon found a horse in the shed saddled and bridled, with the bit hanging out of his mouth so he could munch hay. Patch had evidently brought the horse before heading down to guard the big herd.

Before taking the saddle off the horse in order to get the blanket with which to cover himself, Condon went to the door of the shed for a last look around. He was disturbed to see Vern Gregory walking with a determined stride from the corrals directly to Emma's door. Gregory didn't stop to knock, but barged in, slamming the door behind him.

Uneasy, Cliff crept to the house and peered through the curtains into the living room. The window was partly open, admitting the cool night air, and he could hear plainly what was said. At first he could not see Emma and

124

Vern Gregory, as they were too far to one side, but Gregory was talking in a grim, taunting voice.

'I want that letter, Emma.'

'Who said there was a letter?' Emma replied defiantly.

'Mex Embozo said you got three letters. I know one was for Maxine from Denver, and one was for Mex Embozo. Where's the other letter?'

Condon was perplexed at the tone of the argument. There was no exchange between master and servant; this was a meeting of equals. In what way could Emma Beyer be an equal of Vern Gregory? She was a coarse, strong woman of uneducated speech. Gregory was a gentleman in the accepted sense of the word, educated, charming when it pleased him, but with a hard core of hate in him—hate against the Yankees.

'I burned it!' Emma said.

'You burned it? You're in this as much as I am—it was your idea in the beginning. You wanted a queen, and I've given you one. I want my pay.'

'So you can take her away from here? I want a queen for the Massacre, not one to feed your vanity—not a weapon you can use to get your revenge.'

'Did you think I would stay here forever?' Gregory raised his voice in anger. 'Once I get rid of these cattle and have the money to start

125

with, I'll ruin every Yankee I can and bleed him white. Maxine will be my weapon, as you put it. Do you think I'm going to let you stop me now?'

Gregory had moved into the room where Condon could see him, and there was a maniacal expression on his face. He was like a beast stalking prey.

'Stay here, Vern. Use the money to build a good road up the mesa; invite people from Denver or Saint Louis or even Virginia. But let Maxine be a queen on the Massacre.'

'Don't be a fool! I was a young man when I came here, a young man cheated of his inheritance. If I wait longer for revenge, it will be too late. Maxine is a beauty. She'll put most other women to shame, and she will be my passport into high society. She might even marry a governor. I've rotted here long enough—I've waited and built, and now the time has come to collect. What was in that letter, Emma?'

'I don't know.'

'You're lying. You're still protecting that man who called himself Gabler. Why? He's done nothing but upset things. Ace should have killed him, the fool. He's not Gabler; that's what you're trying to hide. Tell me what was in that letter, Emma.' Gregory took a menacing step forward.

'You're trying to scare me, Vern?' Emma asked in a dry voice. She was still out of

126

Condon's line of vision. 'I was in on the whole scheme, yes, but I didn't expect it to turn into murder. I ain't telling you nothing unless you promise to let that man who called himself Gabler live.'

'You'll tell me what I want to know!' Gregory said, and leaped forward.

Condon heard Emma's gasp, and the sobbing moan as her breath was cut off.

'I'll kill you if I have to,' Gregory snarled, 'and I'll kill him the first chance I get!'

Condon waited for nothing more. He cleared the porch with two steps and threw the door open. He had a glimpse of Emma. Her eyes were rolling in her head, and her face was blue with suffocation. Consumed by rage, Gregory ignored the interruption until Condon got an arm under his chin from behind, and jerked his head back so viciously he was forced to let go of Emma, who fell to the floor, moaning and gasping.

'Kill me now, Gregory!' Condon said, putting a knee in Gregory's back and sending him stumbling across the room. Gregory brought up against the wall; bracing himself, he picked up a chair and sent it hurtling across the room. Condon fell to one side, and the chair crashed behind him. He could see no gun on Gregory. He drew out his own gun and threw it across the room.

'You're older, and I'm still crippled,' Condon said, smiling thinly. 'That makes us even.'

Condon closed in and, favoring his right side, threw a short jab to Gregory's jaw. Strangely, the blow seemed to knock the haze of fury from Gregory's eyes. He shook his head. His breath hissed between his teeth. He was taller than Condon, had a greater reach. For one moment they stood toe to toe trading punches, and Condon suddenly realized that he was up against a trained antagonist. Throwing up his arm, he warded off the rain of blows; then, lurching to the right, he managed to get another hard left hook to Gregory's grim mouth. Blood spurted, and a growl of rage followed it.

Condon felt his head rocked by the swift, vicious punches, and felt the smear of blood on his own lips. Gregory had his guard up, and Condon struck him in his lean stomach. Every blow brought a grunt of pain. While he had Gregory off balance, he kept pounding him until his guard came down. Then he beat and lashed and cut his face. In desperation, Gregory brought up his booted foot and smashed it into Condon's groin. In a red haze of pain, Condon fell to one knee. The low blow had spun him half around, so that his eyes were off Gregory. He heard Emma's choking, garbled cry.

'Look out, Cliff!'

From somewhere on his person Gregory had produced a derringer—a small, ugly gun, as effective as a cannon at close range.

'You asked for killing, and you'll get it!' Gregory snarled.

In Condon all the hurt, the frustration, the futility of his efforts on the Massacre boiled up in his throat. He was tagged for killing; why not now? He barged forward as though the gun didn't exist, as though the one big slug it was ready to cough up had no menace for him.

The very audacity of his charge into the face of certain death unsteadied Gregory's arm, and the bullet missed. Then Condon forgot his wound, and remembered only that Gregory meant to kill him. He beat and pounded the thing before him that looked like a face, the thing that became moist and red and shiny with dripping blood. The blackened eyes were vacant discs as Gregory slid to the floor and lay still. Even then Cliff wouldn't have stopped had not Emma caught his arm.

'Don't kill him—don't kill him,' she pleaded.

Through the stupor of rage Condon looked at her as his anger drained from him. 'He would have killed you—he tried to kill me,' he said between sobbing breaths.

'He's not altogether to blame,' Emma said. 'Let God judge him, Cliff.'

'He's dangerous. Why do you oppose him? I thought you were his servant.'

129

'It's a long story. Some day you might hear it, but not from me. Get on your horse and ride out; forget all that happened here. There's only one thing I ask: take Naomi with you.'

'I'll have to find Naomi. She's out there with Ace on the prowl. She may never come back. And what about Maxine?'

CHAPTER TEN

'Maxine will survive. Gregory's a gambler; she's his ace in the hole. I'll be the loser all around. There's no need for you to die, or Naomi. Sometimes we are punished for crimes we didn't do. Go, before Gregory comes to.'

'I can't leave the Massacre, you know that. If necessary I would die to protect Naomi, but I can't run away with my tail between my legs. I've got a bigger stake here than you think, bigger than cattle and bounty. My brother is one of Gregory's men!'

With that he retrieved his gun and went to the shed, mounted his horse, and rode into the cold, cheerless moonlight.

Tired, sore from the effects of the beating he had taken, his wounded side a dull throb, Condon headed south in the general direction of his last camp. His disguise as Tex had served its purpose; now if he could only contrive to turn Tex loose without too much trouble. He was still riding Tex's rig, although he had a fresh horse, and Tex's rifle was still in the boot.

He had lost all track of time when he approached the ledge in the moonlight. He pulled his horse to a slow walk as he neared the spot where he had left the cowboy bound. He listened for sounds—sounds of pain, or anger, or cursing—but he heard none. Dismounting, he looked about warily. Tex was gone. Condon felt a prickle of fear. He had Tex's rifle, but he had not taken Tex's hand gun or his gunbelt. Nothing happened. He moved warily on foot, leading the horse and heading back to the place where he had made his camp and staked out Bolo.

When he arrived here, everything was gone. Fury rode him, fury at himself. He had become so eager to join the trail drive he had not stopped to think of the consequences. Now he had lost the big horse a second time. It was evident that Tex had worked himself loose, had found Bolo, had saddled him with Condon's own saddle and had ridden off. Tex couldn't be blamed for that; it was his own fault. Weary from the long day of activity, Condon unsaddled, staked out his horse with the riata that was tied to the saddle and lay down to sleep.

He awoke at the first crack of dawn,

refreshed but sore and stiff. The grub he had gotten at the cook shack was still tied to the saddle, and he foraged in the sack for boiled meat and bread. Munching this, he took the rifle and walked back to where Tex had been tied to look for sign. It was possible that Ace Longest had come across Tex, or had heard him yelling and had turned him loose.

As Condon rounded the far end of the ledge, a bullet crashed into the rock beside him. He leaped back for cover, his eyes pinched in a puzzled frown. That was a six-gun shot. No man with a rifle would use a six-gun for a shot of any distance, not if he wanted to be sure of his prey. Condon swung his rifle up, hoping a shot might stir up his tormentor. If the man who had tried to ambush him had taken Bolo and his saddle, he would also have a rifle. If it were Ace Longest, he would also have a rifle of his own. Yet this man had used a six-gun.

'Hello out there!' Condon called.

For answer another forty-five slug sledge-hammered into the rock close to him. Still he held his fire, because he had to make every shot count, having no extra rifle slugs.

'I figgered you'd come back, hombre,' a gravelly voice said from a pile of brush and rocks a hundred yards away. 'I said to myself, that hombre will sure come back looking for me. Ain't no man hogtying me an' settin' me afoot 'thout he pays for it.'

132

'Reckon I deserve it for making such a sloppy job of hogtying.'

'It weren't no sloppy job.'

'You got loose.'

'Some old jasper I ain't seen before turned me loose.'

Condon pondered this. So Cal Moses *had* followed him and kept a watch. 'Where's my horse and rig?' he asked.

'I never seen it.'

'You're the man named Tex, aren't you?'

'Tex Lowman. Wish I was back in Texas. How I ever got euchered into this job, I don't know. You hogtying me last night didn't make me very happy.'

'Saved you a lot of work. Colt Denger sent me out to ride night herd the minute I got there. You had a chance to lie here nice and peaceful. I came back to apologize, but I really did you a favor.'

'Some favor. I reckon I ought to take a shot at you, or beat you up, or something. It ain't manful to be took in like I was and not get some blood or skin to even up.'

'I've got a rifle,' Condon said. 'You can't shootmatch me. I'm too bushed to take on another fight. I beat up Vern Gregory last night.'

'You what?'

'It's a long story. He's going to be after me, dogs and all. I can't stand here palavering all day.'

133

'So you really beat up that highfalutin buzzard? He figgers a waddie like me ain't fit to spit on. I kinda like your style. Got any grub?'

'That I have.'

'What's your proposition?'

'Throw out your gun and come forward, hands up. I'll give you back your saddle, your rifle and a horse to ride if you won't tell Gregory where I am.'

'I wouldn't tell him nothing. Anyways. I don't aim to look like a fool by talking about being ambushed. Where was I supposed to be last night?'

'Night-hawking the big herd. I never found where it was.'

Condon didn't explain about the help he'd gotten from Gust Allen, for to expose the big Negro's part in his escape would only put Patch in bad with Vern Gregory.

'You got yourself a deal, mister,' Tex said, tossing out his six-gun. A moment later there emerged from the brush a bowlegged cowboy, hair red as cayenne, and with a host of freckles mottling his face. He had gray eyes and lean jaws, he was about Cliff's height, but his long arms and legs made him look scrawny. He looked about warily, like a man used to being trailed.

'Hold it there, Tex, until I get your gun.'

'Suspicious feller, ain't you? Reckon a Texan don't like his word being took lightly.'

'A crook I don't trust, regardless where he's from,' Cliff said, striding forward and picking up the gun.

'I didn't figure to be no crook. I was long-ropin' just enough dogies to start me a herd, like all them bit shots done to get going. I was talked into this Massacre caper, and it looked like a dead sure thing. I ain't so sure now. Gregory keeps yakking how much we're each going to get in the showdown, but I reckon he'll keep most of the dinero hisself.'

'Did you expect him to give it to you? Come on up the other side of the ledge there, over that hump.'

Back at the camp, Condon let Tex help himself to what grub was in the sack. Then they exchanged hats and coats.

'How did you get up here from Texas? Did you come by way of Mescosa?'

'Sure did. That's where I heard of the Massacre, and got interested.'

'Is there a man there named Kile?'

'Kile *is* Mescosa. He's got more connections than a webby spider. Supplies beef to the reservations, the army posts—even as far as Santa Fe. He uses up a right healthy amount of cattle. With the drought in New Mexico and Arizona, a man with cattle can name his own price, almost,' Tex said. 'You're all-fired full of questions, pardner. What's your name?'

Condon saw no harm in continuing the lie

135

he had started. 'My name's Gabler, Carl Gabler.'

Tex looked at him with wary eyes. 'If you is Gabler, then my name's Jehoshaphat. I drank with Gabler in Mescosa. He's supposed to come up here repping for Kile, but you ain't him. What's your game?'

Condon took a liking to this cowboy, who was too naïve to be a real crook and too eager to get ahead to tread the straight and narrow. Because there was little else he could do, he decided to trust him with the truth. In as few words as he could, Condon told Tex how he had come to the Massacre, about the two men he meant to bring to justice, how Naomi had befriended him and Ace was out to kill him.

'Man, you sure got yourself a job. How you going to do anything by yourself alone?' Tex said, whistling through his teeth.

'No man's alone, Tex,' Cliff said quietly. 'Already I've got four people on my side, maybe five.'

'But none of them people can help you much. I could do more than all of them put together.'

'What do you mean?'

'I ain't interested in your bounty bait or your personal revenge. Them things can get a man in trouble. Gettin' your cows back, that's a different proposition.'

'Yeah? I don't even know a trail off the Massacre a cow could travel. I practically climbed up hand over fist,' Condon said.

'You saw us rawhidin' that bunch last night from the south?'

'I couldn't find a trail there. Nothing but a scramble path.'

'If you had a hoss, I'd show you something. Maybe you and me could work together and cut some of the gravy out from under Gregory.'

'Talk sense, Tex.'

'There's a small herd, about a thousand head, in Mud Springs Flat, due east of here. It's a day's ride from the bunkhouse, so a couple of riders stay out there with the herd four days at a time. If I got to night-hawkin' that herd, I could head 'em over this way and take them off the mesa the way we come up last night. There's a water seep in a box canyon near Nos Pes where we could hide them until the chase was over and then split them up.'

'You've got more enthusiasm than sense, Tex. You couldn't handle that bunch of cattle . . .'

'With your help—and the girl Naomi— maybe even the old geezer who turned me loose last night would give a hand. Ain't none of them in love with Gregory.'

Condon shook his head doubtfully, but he had to elicit any help he could, and Tex's plan at least would create a diversion.

'When you need help, holler,' he said.

'You'd better get going. Here's your hand-gun and your rifle, loaded. Take the horse and get out. I think I know where my horse is.'

Condon watched the young cowboy ride away and shook his head. Turning, he started for the Hucklebreck line shack on foot.

It was after the noon hour when he topped a wooded knoll and sat down to rest his burning feet. Hunger began gnawing at his guts, but he cinched up his belt, licking the dust off his dry lips. He should have taken the canteen from Tex's saddle, but he had already made so much trouble for the cowboy, he felt obliged to him. There would be water at the line shack, but by that time his throat would be raw and his feet a torture.

'Things ain't that bad, son,' the voice of Cal Moses said from right behind him. It was as though the old man were reading his thoughts.

Condon sighed, but he didn't turn his head. 'I reckon I'm easier caught than a bullfrog in a mud pond. It wouldn't take any dogs to track me.'

'Don't fret yourself, Cliff.'

'Do you know my name?'

'Naomi told me all about you. I like your spirit, but I doubt your wisdom. I saw you coming from four ridges away and figured I'd catch up with you here.' The older man became suddenly talkative. 'Gregory's got the dogs out, so you better stay away from the shack until he brings them in for the night—if he brings them in.'

A faint nicker caused Condon to turn his head, and he saw, to his delight, that Cal Moses had brought Bolo. He leaped up, forgetting the soreness of his feet, and threw his arms around the big paint horse's neck. He rubbed his stubbled chin against the velvet muzzle.

'I'm sure glad to see you, boy!' he exclaimed. Then he looked at Moses. 'Where did you find him?'

'Where you left him. I found the cowboy you hogtied. Turned him loose.'

'How come he didn't take Bolo from you? He was armed.'

'I had hidden the horse. The cowboy thought I was an apparition and was glad to see me go. Your horse is all right; you did a good job of sticking him. Better watch his feed, though. There's grub in your saddle bag, and water in the can.'

'Did you speak to Gregory?'

'I never speak with him. I saw him from a distance. His face is raw and branded. He has death in his heart, death for you. You got two men now, Ace and Gregory, each carrying a bullet with your name on it. There ain't a doubt you're going to die, just who's going to kill you. It might be the dogs.'

'They can't trail me,' Condon said grimly.

'If he puts them on the trail of the cayuse I rode from Emma's shed last night, they'll follow it to where I gave the horse back to Tex, and trail him back to the ranch.'

'That's a probability. But Gregory won't give up—he might give up everything else, but he'll get his revenge. Even if he moves the cattle, he'll never leave the Massacre with you alive.'

'I'm not a killing man, Moses, but I don't die easy, either.'

'You owe your life twice already—maybe three times.'

'How do you mean, three times?'

'Ace missed that first shot. He won't miss a second time. If Gregory ain't back to the line shack by dark, it means he's going to keep the dogs out all night,' Moses said.

'What good are they at night, if they glow? They can be seen by the man they're after.'

'Only part of them glow, Cliff. The ones who glow can lead you right into the jaws of the killer dogs. Naomi doesn't want you dead. Come to the line shack after dark; it will be the safest place.'

'Thank you, Moses. Some day I'll repay you.'

'Pray for me.'

Condon watched the tall, straight figure of the older man fade silently into the trees. He washed the dust and dryness from his throat with water from the canteen, and ate hungrily

140

of the jerky and sourdough bread. He remained concealed in the trees where he could watch the country below him, but he continued to see only straying bunches of cattle and dust spirals sucked up by the wind.

Later in the afternoon, his chafed feet rested, he mounted the big pinto horse and rode cautiously toward the line shack. 'You must be hungry, boy,' Cal greeted him.

'Not too hungry, thanks to the jerky and sourdough you fetched me.'

'I expected you. I made some rabbit stew. Naomi tells me it tastes very good.'

Moses went to the corner bench and scrubbed his hands.

The hot stew *was* good, and a welcome relief from stale bread and hard meat. Condon knew better than to offer Moses the stew. The older man ate some beans and raw carrots, but not until he had muttered a sibilant prayer. After black coffee, they washed the tin dishes and pushed the stew pot off the fire.

'I'd better get out of here before the dogs come,' Condon suggested.

'They can be heard far off. Set easy. You're getting yourself in a worse fix all the time,' Moses said, shaking his head. 'What can you do now? If you show yourself anywhere, Gregory will hear about it.'

'I don't know what I can do, but I can keep trying.' He told about Tex Lowman's proposition, and Moses shook his head again.

'If such a fool plan could work, you'd have your cattle, but you wouldn't have your men. Are five hundred cattle worth your life?'

Condon knew that the cattle had become secondary, and that the most Tex's scheme could do would be create a diversion. There were killers to be caught, and there was his brother Arny to be saved. At last a plan formed in his mind.

'Can I use your tablet and pencil, Moses?'

'Reckon so,' the older man said, taking the tablet off the shelf over the table. He fumbled for a stub of pencil.

Moving into the circle of candlelight, Condon wrote:

Sheriff Vinson: Found cattle and killers. Big drive to river soon south of Hanker. Bring U.S. marshal and lawmen from looted ranges. Barges due soon. Condon.

'What you aim to do with that?' Moses asked.

'Wire it from Tooker. Naomi can sneak it out for me.'

'Do you think she can make the operator at Tooker send the wire?'

'He's bound by law to send any wire that's paid for.'

'Do you think he'll keep his mouth shut?'

'That's a chance I've got to take,' Condon

said grimly.

Condon slept in the shed; he was awakened by a hand shaking him when dawn was still a dim promise in the eastern sky. Though he couldn't see her face in the dim light, Condon knew Naomi stood over him.

'You'd better get up and eat breakfast. You've got to leave here. Gregory brought the dogs home late last night; kept them in a corral. He'll be coming this way next. He's like a maniac. No man has ever laid a hand on him before, and you cut him up bad. What makes it worse, he's got to face Clay Jordan.'

'Clay Jordan?' Condon frowned. 'Who is he?'

'He's one of Maxine's men friends from Denver. Owns a mine or something. He kept writing to Maxine, and she didn't answer. Yesterday he showed up, vowing to marry her. Sometimes Vern acts as though he's jealous, as though he doesn't want Maxine to marry at all. Clay Jordan isn't man to give up easy. Maybe he'll be the first Gregory cheats to get even with the Yankees.'

'What does Maxine say about it?'

'She's acting coy, stringing him along. It's silly how much a man wants something he can't have. She's not giving him any easy kisses, but she'll marry him, if I'm any judge of Maxine. She could be queen of Denver then. Vern might even get enough money to buy back his Virginia home. We haven't got time to stand here and gabble.'

Washing the sleep out of his eyes at the water trough, Condon followed Naomi to the house. Moses was gone.

'You'll have to finish the stew,' she said, pulling it over the fire. 'These coffee grounds have probably been used three times, but they still have color in them.'

While he ate, they told each other of the things that had happened to them since their last meeting. He put his arms around her when he rose from the table. 'There is justice in the world, Naomi. Sometimes it takes a long time to show itself, but like evil it grows and grows, until the fruit ripens. The fruit of evil is death, and the fruit of justice is life.'

'How is it going to end, Cliff?'

'Will you do one thing more for me?'

'If I can.'

'Have you ever been to Tooker?'

'Not lately.'

'Could you get to Tooker?'

'I can get anywhere I want. Why?'

He showed her the note he had written. 'Would you send this wire for me?'

She read it and looked up at him. 'This would destroy the Massacre. The Massacre's been my home all of my life. I've grown accustomed to the crookedness and the evil. You ask me to help destroy it?'

'If my plan works, the Massacre will still be here, but the evil will be gone. Do you want to be a slave to Maxine and her father all your life?'

'Will they send the wire?' she asked uncertainly.

'They'll have to send it, if you pay for it. They might get word to Gregory that the wire has been sent, but that won't help him much. I'd go myself, but I'd never make it, and if I did, I would be locked up. I'm sure Gregory has put out a warrant for me.'

'I'll try to send it,' she said simply.

In spite of all his troubles, Cliff still had his money in his money belt. Nobody had tried to rob him. He gave her the note and some money which she put in the pocket of her denim jacket.

'I'll saddle my horse and ride out with you, Naomi.'

They rode from the stockade together, and for some distance they were hidden by the trees. Then, where the trail north turned off across a swale, they parted, and Naomi rode on alone. Condon watched her from his shelter in the trees.

Naomi was almost across the open space when out of the trees raced the dogs, heading for the line shack which was their home. After them came Patch on a big black horse, and Vern Gregory on a blooded thoroughbred. Gregory saw Naomi and shouted at her. There was a short conversation. Condon could not hear the words, but he saw Naomi swerve her pony as though to ride around the two men. Gregory shouted at her again, and then spun the thoroughbred to cut her off. Naomi's pony was no match for the long-legged thoroughbred. Gregory caught her and dragged her from the saddle. He rolled from the saddle with her, and when she rose to her knees he began searching her pockets. Naomi, still stunned by the sudden attack, knelt before him while he drew out the message and read it.

Condon, seeing the girl's danger, rode from the trees to rescue her. His own safety meant nothing to him now. Even as he rode across the swale, he heard Gregory scream:

'You dirty little traitor!'

Then the bullwhip he used on the dogs rose and fell in his hand. The lash beat and cut into the girl's back. Condon's eyes swam red with the fury that consumed him. Everything was happening so fast. Patch was off his horse in one great leap. He threw himself over the girl, taking the sting of the deadly thongs upon his own back.

'Drop that whip, Gregory, or I'll kill you!' Condon shouted.

Gregory heard nothing but the crack of the whip, saw nothing but the victims before him. Condon jerked his horse to a stop and pulled the rifle from the boot in the same motion. The big pinto knew when to stand deathly still as Condon took aim. Condon muttered a prayer and squeezed the trigger. The whip went flying through the air, and Gregory was spun around like a drunken scarecrow.

CHAPTER ELEVEN

Gregory was down on his knees, holding his bleeding arm and sobbing in impotent rage, when Condon reached the group. His bloodshot eyes blazed glassily through the tears that blinded him.

Condon knelt at Naomi's side. His jaw hardened as he saw how the thongs had cut through the material of her jacket.

'Get him out of here, Patch. Take him to Emma before he bleeds to death.'

'Ah got to fix up that arm some way, now,' Patch said, shaking his head and fumbling at the bandana around his throat.

Naomi lifted her face, and there was no hate in it, no anger; just pity and understanding.

'I'll bandage his arm, Patch.'

'He whupped you like a dog, chile.'

'He didn't know what he was doing.'

Marveling at the girl's depth of feeling, Condon helped her to her feet. She went to Gregory, took Patch's handkerchief and tied it tightly above the wound to stop the flow of blood. Then, finding a clean handkerchief in Gregory's riding coat, she bandaged the wound itself.

'This changes nothing,' Gregory said in a flat, deadly voice as he dragged himself aboard the thoroughbred. 'It only adds one more tally to my score against you, Gabler, or whatever your name is. I'm giving orders to every man in the crew to shoot to kill if they see you. Get off the Massacre, or your blood will be on your own head.'

Condon unconsciously put his arm around Naomi as he watched them ride into the trees. He looked into her eyes and kissed her as though it were the most natural thing to do. His lips lingered, and he felt a strange sensation of joy, of expanding power, of doors opening into dark, secret places.

'Naomi, I wonder if there is a man worthy of you. Did they teach you this forbearance at the Mission school? Did they teach you this humility, this God-given strength to turn the other cheek?'

'I'm not as noble as you think, Cliff. To watch a man die when you can save him is murder. I am no murderer, but I am human, and I have feelings of love and hate, sadness and joy. To deprive Gregory of the power and position he is fighting for would be no sin, because he would abuse them at the expense of the others. We can still get your message

148

through.'

'You can't go to Tooker now. Gregory will have you watched; he'll have a man in Tooker to stop you.'

'I'm not going to Tooker. One of the boys from the Mission school can take the message on horseback,' she said.

'Two hundred miles?'

'He could make it there in two days if he could get a fresh horse halfway. There's a trading post at the Hovenweep.'

'It will take you half a day to find the boy,' he objected. Then he told her about Tex and his scheme to steal one of the herds. 'Maybe that could help us,' he finished.

'That still wouldn't stop Gregory, or get you the men you're after. You can't avoid a showdown with Ace—he's one of the men you want. Do you know who the other one is?'

'I'd know him if I saw him. I remember the poster you burned.'

'You *have* seen him. He's Mex Embozo.'

'It was he who saved you from Ace,' Condon said. 'I'm sorry he's the one.'

'Men are not all good or all bad, Cliff. If Mex gets a fair trial, that's all he can expect. I doubt if he'll go with you easily. Do you still think you can get two such men back to Delgado by yourself?'

'I don't know.'

'Send the message. Get help. Kile's barges

may be held up. In the meantime, let Tex try his rustling scheme—help him. That might delay things until other lawmen can get here.'

They rode back to the line shack, where the dogs were prowling about the stockade. They closed the gate and fed the hungry animals, and Condon became aware of how important it was to be friends with them. When the dogs were quieted, they went into the shack, and Condon wrote another note in Moses' tablet. He gave this to Naomi, along with more money from his money belt.

'Give this to your Indian boy, Naomi. He might need it to get a fresh mount. Above all, watch out for yourself. To succeed at your expense would be no victory for me.'

She stood before him, rose on tiptoe and kissed him on the mouth. As she turned to go, she said, 'You'd better not stay here. I'll get in touch with you somehow.' Then she was gone.

Taking more jerky and sourdough bread, Condon filled his canteen and rode away without waiting for Cal Moses to return. He camped at the same water seep he had used before and in the morning was up early and in the saddle.

Reaching the cattle trail, he followed it south into the wild growth of juniper and piñon. He was still at a loss as to how the cattle had been driven to the top of the mesa, for he had found no trail up the cliff but the footpath he had negotiated.

Moving forward warily, fearful of an ambush, Condon approached the bluff, the base of which was choked with rabbit sage, berry bushes and trees. There was a passage in the brush a few feet wide, and then the secret was revealed to him. A cave extended into the face of the cliff, and as he peered into it, he could feel a strong current of air. Dismounting, he entered the cave and found the floor trampled smooth by many hooves. The roof was not high enough to allow a man on horseback, but a man could easily lead his horse inside. Advancing until the daylight from the mouth of the cave was practically exhausted, he discovered he was looking down a long gentle incline at the bottom of which light was visible.

Going back for Bolo, Condon led the big horse into the tunnel and down the almost dark incline to the bottom of the Arroyo Diablo, almost directly across from the spot where he had searched for a trail up the cliff. He recalled now that the water had been high from the cloudburst and had evidently filled the lower entrances to the tunnel. He finally understood why Ace had been patrolling the area around the top of the tunnel.

Mounting, Condon rode down the arroyo in the direction of the river, curious as to how the cattle would be brought down to the barges. He wound his way down the boulder-strewn bottom of the arroyo, through pools of water left by the storm, and past rattlesnakes that basked on the hot rocks. By noon the sun poured into the narrow cavity like molten brass. Condon dared not shoot the snakes, for a gun-shot here would echo and travel like a thunderbolt.

The cliffs on the mesa side were like walls, gashed and eroded by the cruel thrusts of wind and rain, but practically insurmountable. Somewhere near the river, they had to level off to provide a trail. The cattle could go down by the wagon road that led to Hanker, but this would prove a slow and tedious method of loading the barges. Once the operation got under way, any delay would prove disastrous. Cattle had to eat, and there was little forage along the river; nothing but sand and stone and gnarled trees.

He stopped at a pool to eat, and let his horse drink his fill. The water in the rocky basin was clear and pure and no range man left such water without filling his canteen. Later in the afternoon, Condon saw another almost impossible trail leading up the wall of the mesa to a natural shelf about halfway to the top. It was not a trail for cattle, but a shod horse could make the climb. Taking advantage of every clue, Condon decided to inspect the shelf. It might possibly spiral around the breast of the mesa and provide an access to the river.

Leading Bolo, as he had done before, Condon crawled and scrambled up the rough path. Once Bolo lost his footing and almost went crashing into the arroyo, but luckily his sharp iron shoes caught on a riffle in the rock and saved him. The sun was setting by the time they reached the shelf, or what had looked like a shelf from below. Instead of a shelf, it was a wide expanse of grazing ground, a half-mile across and longer than Condon could see. There were cattle grazing here, and in the approximate center of the range was a thick growth of aspen and cotton-woods that marked the presence of water. It was a beautiful spot, a veritable Eden for a cattle-minded man. It was not big enough to sustain a large herd, but it would keep a thousand head for weeks.

Condon frowned. This was the isolated pasture Tex had spoken of; it had to be. It was on the east edge of the mesa. The cattle roaming the grass and brush-covered land were the cattle Tex meant to steal. Condon climbed into the saddle and studied the country. There had to be access to this place from the top of the mesa, and if there was, there might be a passage from this shelf down to the river.

Riding warily, Condon approached the center of the flat, where the indications of water promised a comfortable camp. There he found the remains of other camps, some of them recent, and realized that this spot was used as headquarters for the men who guarded the isolated herd of cattle. Watering his horse and covering his tracks as best he could, Condon retreated from the waterhole into the trees until he felt sufficiently concealed. There he settled down to chew hard meat and stale bread, washed down with water.

It was dark when two men rode into the clearing at the waterhole. Condon was not surprised to see Tex, but he was surprised when he saw the golden horse and silver-mounted saddle of Mex Embozo, and Mex Embozo himself.

The two men built a fire, and while one of them plucked and eviscerated two sage hens they had shot, the other filled a pot with water and put it over the fire, preparatory to making coffee. Condon's mouth watered as the smell of roasting meat and boiling coffee wafted his way to plague him.

Then, to add to Condon's dismay, his brother Arny rode into the circle of light. With the bright flames lighting his face, there was no doubt about the man's identity. The sight sickened Condon, and a shudder ran through his lean body. Where had he failed Arny? What had he done wrong that would turn his younger brother to the owlhoot trail? Arny had been mischievous and wild as a boy, but such energies are usually channeled

154

into normal activities as a boy grows older. Here was Arny allied with the men who had robbed the Delgado range and killed Hal Chester. He had been a friend to both him and Arny, and that Arny should condone such a crime was beyond understanding.

Yet Condon dared not show himself. To invite gunplay would be disastrous and inconclusive, no matter who got killed. All he could do was spy helplessly and pray that Naomi's Indian messenger got through in time. When the meal was over, the three men rolled smokes, which they enjoyed over a final cup of coffee, all the while carrying on a lengthy discussion. Finally Mex Embozo and Arny got up and rode into the darkness, while Tex spread his blanket for a nap before starting the night watch.

On impulse, Condon crept closer to the fire and called out in a low voice, 'Tex—this is Condon.'

The redhead spun around, his gun leveled, and saw Condon with his hands above his head.

'Don't never sneak up on a Texan like that in the dark,' he said. 'How did you find this place without being killed?'

'By looking for it. I've got to talk to you.'

'I ain't sure I want to talk to you. You're getting to be a hoodoo for sure. Beating Gregory up was bad enough, and he was content to get revenge in person. Now that you shot his arm—his gun arm so he can't use it—he's offering a thousand dollars to the man who brings you to him.'

'All right, take me in and get your thousand dollars.'

'I ain't no bounty buzzard; they're worse than coyotes.'

Condon thought of Mex Embozo, who had just left, of the bounty on his head and of his own determination to bring Embozo back to Delgado.

Dropping his hands, but keeping them clear of his gun, he said, 'What were you hombres talking about? Before you tell me, I might tell you that I found the tunnel trail off the mesa.'

'This rustling job is too big for you and me. I was feeling them out about joining us,' Tex replied.

'What did they say?'

'They've got to have time to make up their minds.'

'If they're coming in on it, you'll have to take more cattle to make it pay off.'

'We can pick up another thousand along the way.'

'Don't you think it was dangerous to tell them?'

'The Mex won't squeal on me. The other hombre is a new man, but he looks smart enough to keep his mouth shut. Mex will see to that.'

156

'You didn't bring up my name, did you?'

'No. If they don't string along, I'll still need you, Condon.'

'When you going to push the cattle out of here?'

'Tomorrow night or the next night. I'll let Naomi know.'

Condon thought quickly. If Mex Embozo came along with the herd, he would still be within his reach. If he got the five hundred cattle back and put Mex Embozo safely behind bars in Nos Pes, that would leave only Ace Longest, and he could return for him.

'Try to get Mex to go with us; we could use the help,' Condon said.

'I need forty winks before I take my turn, midnight to dawn. You'll hear from me.'

Condon liked the young Texan. He put out his hand and felt the pressure of the redhead's fingers.

Condon decided against sleeping near the waterhole, because in the daylight he might not be able to get away without being spotted. He put the bit back into Bolo's mouth and rode north across the wide benchland, trusting to his horse to pick the way. When he reached a broken country where the junipers began to thicken, he stopped to sleep.

Dawn awoke him after three hours of sound sleep—not much but enough to relax his muscles and sharpen his wits.

Warily, he turned his horse up the trail from the bench to the top of the mesa. Cautiously peering over the rim, he saw a vast flat covered with cattle. So this was the herd he was supposed to have night-hawked the night he had beaten up Gregory. It was difficult to estimate the number of cattle. They had cropped the grass almost to the roots, and would soon have to be moved.

Condon skirted the flat, caution impeding his progress until he was around the herd. Then, through the broken, wooded country, he took the shortest trail possible toward the line shack. At dark he approached cautiously and was amazed when the dogs made no outcry. Even at the approach of a friend, they usually set up a noisy greeting.

He opened the gate to the stockade and found the dogs there, busy with an extra feeding of meat. They snarled softly or growled over their portions, looking like luminescent ghosts in the dark. They did not dispute his presence, but suffered his caresses without complaint. He put his horse in the shed, fed him an extra portion of grain and closed the bin tightly. Then he went back to the shack.

Cal Moses was there, writing in the thick tablet, which he closed and put on the shelf at Condon's entry.

'Don't let me disturb your writing,' Cliff said.

Moses turned.

'A man puts words on paper to scourge them from his soul. I have all eternity for writing. I saw you out there waiting for the dark. I fed the dogs to keep them quiet. I hoped you had gone from the mesa, but I knew you'd be back.'

'Has Naomi been here since I left?'

'No. She may have taken your message herself.'

'I hope not. She's the only contact I have with Gregory now. I talked to Tex last night. He's still planning on running off the herd on the bench. He might not make it, but it will keep Gregory from getting the big herd away before the men I sent for get here. I can help Tex.'

Moses shook his hairy head. 'Stubbornness is for mules, Cliff. Why don't you go after some lawmen yourself? You can trail the men you want, even if they have left the Massacre.'

'Once Ace Longest and Mex Embozo leave here, I could trail them for years. I've got my brother to save—he's one of the rustlers. As for the cattle, cattle are the life blood of the West. Without cattle, there would be little excuse for living here in this empty, tortured land.'

'May God help you—if there is a God.'

The bitterness in the older man's words disturbed Cliff.

'They tell me God helps those who help themselves, Moses,' he said.

Naomi did not come that night. Cliff slept in the shed and left the stockade before daylight, after eating a cold breakfast. Cal Moses was already gone. Condon resumed his watch from the trees a quarter of a mile from the cabin, determined to talk to Naomi the minute she arrived.

Near noon, a lone rider came from the trees across the swale and headed for the cabin, the swift beat of the horse's feet sending puffs of dust into the bright sunshine. Condon recognized the horse before he recognized the rider. There was no mistaking Silver, Maxine's horse. Condon mounted and reached the stockade ahead of her. Why had she come there—she who had expressed her revulsion and fear of Cal Moses? He was glad the older man was not around to face her arrogant disdain.

Maxine's face was almost expressionless when she stopped before him. 'I had to see you,' she said simply, and added with finality, 'once more.'

'You're not sent here as bait to lure me into Gregory's trap?'

'Gregory is like a strange, haunted man. You did it to him.'

'I defended Emma, and I defended Naomi against him. If that's evil, then I'm a sinner, but remember that I could have hurt him much worse. I could have killed him!'

'I haven't come to plead his cause, but my own, Cliff. Is that crazy old man here?'

'You mean Cal Moses?'

'You know who I mean.'

'He is gone. We can't stay here. I'm in danger.'

'Come inside; nobody will bother us today,' she said, leading her horse into the corral and speaking softly to the dogs.

Condon followed her into the yard, where they ground-dallied their mounts; then they entered the cabin.

'Why have you come?' he asked.

'I'm called the mistress of Massacre—the queen of the mesa. I get my way because my father, Vern Gregory, pleases to humor me, but he means to collect double for every indulgence. I cut quite a swath in Denver not because I'm worthy but because I'm beautiful. More than one man wants me up there, but they're the kind of men who love possessions, whether they be horses, diamonds, or women. The quiet, honest men who could love a woman as a woman are afraid to come near me, afraid of being burned like a moth in a flame.'

'What have I got to do with all that?' Condon protested, aware of her rising emotion.

'You come here! You come here and upset everybody's life—and for different reasons.

161

Emma has turned against my father in order to protect you. Naomi, poor blind Naomi, would die for you, and you pet her like a good dog. You've driven Gregory to the brink of insanity, and you've set the stage for murder. I've got a chance to marry a rich man, a very rich man, but I have to find out if the thing I feel for you every time we meet is real—if it is love or rebellion against Vern.'

'How did you know where to find me?'

'Naomi told me.'

'Did she know why you were coming here?'

'Would you know if somebody stuck a knife in your back? She had to let me come, because she needs to know the truth as well as I.'

'What makes you think you would want me?' he asked. 'I've got a small spread which wouldn't make enough to keep you in clothes and paint.'

'A woman in love can dress in gunnysacks and forget paint. Love means different things to a man and to a woman. When a woman loves a man, she thinks of the children he can give her; she thinks of the security and warmth of a home, not for a day or a month, but forever. A man has his security built within him, and for him a woman can be an incident, a passing fancy, or she can mean responsibility and dedication.'

'Love needs no debate, no explanation,' he retorted. 'Love exists because it's there; it has no shape or form or reason. If it must be analyzed, it is not whole. Love is the mortar that holds a stone wall together. You can smash the wall, blast it to bits, but the mortar clings to the stone.'

'Don't preach to me—kiss me!' she said, her face turned up to his, pleading and expectant.

Unclenching his hands, he put his arms around her and let his lips cling to hers. When he released her, she let her arms fall at her sides. As she stepped back, he realized where his love lay: not with selfishness and pride, but with gentleness and devotion.

Maxine stood there, shaken and defeated. Her eyes were glassy with unshed tears. She had gotten her answer, one she was impotent to change. There *was* something in life she could not have for the taking. Finding no words to express the confusion within her, she walked silently from the cabin. Condon hadn't the courage to follow her, or the will. Whatever he might say would compound her defeat. He heard her ride from the stockade and the gate slam shut behind her.

CHAPTER TWELVE

After waiting until Maxine was out of sight, Condon rode from the stockade to his hideaway in the trees. It was still hours before dark, and he decided to catch up on some sleep in case he had another busy night. If Naomi did not find him at the cabin, he felt sure she would look here where they had watched the trail before. He staked out his horse on the best graze, and then fell into a welcome sleep.

He sensed her presence before she spoke, and he opened his eyes to see her silhouetted against the twilight. Her face was blank, and her manner stiff and strange. She fumbled inside her shirt and held out her hand.

'Take your badge; you're going to need it.'

Their hands touched, and she jerked hers away as he took the badge, as though the contact had burned her.

'What's the matter, Naomi? Did you see Maxine?'

'I met her on the trail.'

'Why did you send her here to me?'

'I didn't send her; I told her where to find you. I see she did find you.'

'You act as though I did something wrong. What is it, Naomi?'

'You couldn't help yourself. Maxine is bait no man can resist, Cliff. I'm not blaming you; I'm blaming myself for not seeing the truth.'

'What did Maxine tell you?' Cliff demanded, suspecting what was wrong.

'She didn't have to tell me in words. I saw it in her eyes, in the way she looked at me.

She pitied me.'

'It could have been a look of envy, Naomi.'

'Why lie to me? The evidence is on your face; you should have washed it.'

Condon rubbed his hand across his mouth, and it came away red with the residue from Maxine's lips.

'She came to learn the truth about herself. I kissed her, and that kiss proved the truth to her and to me.' Condon pleaded for understanding, but the implacable expression did not leave her eyes.

'We have no time to argue about love. There is too much hate to be destroyed right now, tonight; before the next day is over there may be nothing left to love.'

'What do you mean, Naomi?'

'The barges have come. Before dawn the cattle will be moving for the river.'

Condon knew what this meant. Unless some way could be found to interfere with the movement of the cattle, it would be all over and he would be empty-handed. There was still a chance.

'I've got to get down to the bench and alert Tex to start pushing the cattle he intends to rustle up toward the cave,' he said quickly, his mind racing.

Her next words stopped his mind dead in its tracks; it made his body a sickened, trembling thing.

'Tex is dead!' she shouted the word.

165

'What did you say?' he managed to form the words.

'He's dead—dead—dead!'

'No—no, he can't be dead. I saw him last night.'

'Somebody gave him away—somebody told Gregory what he was planning. Gregory sent Colt Denger to kill him, knowing Tex wouldn't have a chance in a shootout,' Naomi said in a bitter voice. 'What do you intend to do now, lawman?'

Through the fog of disbelief that isolated him for the moment, Cliff remembered Mex Embozo and Arny, his brother at the fire with Tex. He recalled Tex's reassuring words, 'Mex won't squeal on me.' If Mex had not squealed on him, that left only Arny. Where could Arny ever find redemption now? Cliff shook off the paralysis that held him helpless and turned to the waiting girl.

'I want you to believe one thing, Naomi, before it's too late to tell you. I love you. That's the lesson I learned from Maxine's kiss—that's the lesson she took away with her. What you saw in her expression when you met her on the trail was not triumph for herself and pity for you; it was just the opposite. Will you help me tonight?'

'Do you have to ask that, Cliff? What are we going to do?'

'We're going to take the dogs out to the edge of the mesa above the barges. And when the cattle start down those steep trails to the river, we're going to stampede them. Once they start down, nothing or nobody can stop them. They will run through the river, smash over the barges. They will scatter into the broken country beyond the river, and it will take days to gather them. By that time your Indian will have delivered the note and the help I hope for may have arrived.'

'That's a long chance, Cliff. People are going to die. I don't want you to die.'

'I'll take a lot of killing. It's you I'm worried about. You can't be in on the stampede.'

'You need me. We've got to come in from two sides, with dogs yowling and guns blasting, if you're going to head the herd down the bank. Who else can you get to help you?'

'Cal Moses. He's peculiar in many ways, but he believes in what's right—above everything he believes in what's right. I don't know what he's scribbling in that tablet; it may be another Bible.'

'It may be a confession, Cliff. He didn't always live on the mesa, I'm sure of that.'

'It's a long track to the loading point, but we can make it following the trail I took to get here yesterday. Will the dogs go with us?'

'The dogs will follow me,' she said confidently.

'Let's get back to the line shack and see if

167

Moses is back.'

She stood before him, her face still upturned and a question still in her eyes. Condon looked at her and saw the courage, the sacrifice and the strength that were waiting for him to claim. His long arms went about her and he pressed her to him, claiming her lips not in swift passion, but in a lingering embrace that promised much more—so much more than Maxine could ever give. Without a word they mounted and rode back to the line shack.

Cal Moses was sitting there without a light, his big body a mere shadow in the gloom. The fire on the fireplace was a bed of coals, over which hung the pots of food and coffee.

'We had better eat before we go,' he said as though reading their minds.

Without explanation Condon said, 'You'll help us?' How Cal Moses knew what trouble and tragedy the night promised he didn't know.

'You're a man of purpose, Cliff Condon, and persistence. I've known all along it would end like this. When a man refuses to sacrifice an ounce of courage, an inch of integrity, a morsel of pride, at least he dies pure. I wish to God I had had the courage. Perhaps this night I shall make my atonement.'

Cliff explained his plan for stampeding the cattle. Moses nodded his head. 'It is a plan, but not a simple one. Somebody will have to die. Who will it be? You? Me? Naomi? Or will it be Gregory, the straw man?' Moses said.

Condon, puzzled by the older man's remarks, made no effort to interpret them. Moses was a man unto himself, whose mind wandered into weird, remembered places that haunted him.

'You have no horse, Moses,' Condon said.

'I can outwalk your horse over a distance.'

'But you can't get caught in a stampede on foot.'

'I shall be provided for,' Moses said mysteriously.

They finished eating and prepared to leave. In the shed were muzzles and long leashes Gregory used on the dogs for training or to restrain them from killing when there was no need for killing. Moses took four of the dogs, but refused to carry a gun. Naomi took the other four dogs, dallied to the pommel of her saddle. She had her gun. Cliff had his gun and rifle. They set out, the dogs eerily luminous in the dark. There would be little danger from lookouts; the men would all be too busy handling the cattle.

'They're bringing the cattle down on three different days, about two or three thousand in each group. It will take all the men to handle the cattle being loaded. The other cattle will be near the edge of the mesa, waiting their turn to go down, but there will be only one or two men with them,' Naomi explained.

'If we stampede the first group, they can't load the others until the barges are repaired and the cattle rounded up,' Condon said grimly.

*   *   *

When they reached the north edge of the mesa below which the barges waited, Condon called a halt. Although it was not yet light, up ahead there was already noise and confusion. Gregory had not waited for daylight. Condon felt the cold hand of defeat reaching out to him. There was no time to lose. They were passing another quiet herd, which would be the second one over the edge of the mesa and down the steep trails.

Turning to Naomi, Condon said, 'Give me the dogs. You ride on home and keep an eye on things at the ranch.'

'I came to help you,' Naomi insisted.

Condon knew if anything happened to her, he would never forgive himself. He had to send her out of danger.

'You can help best by keeping an eye on things at the ranch,' he repeated.

'Here; take the dogs,' she said.

Surprised at her quick surrender, Condon took the leashes she unwound from her pommel. 'Take care of yourself,' he cautioned her. 'Remember I love you.'

'You take care of yourself,' she retorted as she rode away and there was a determination in her voice that made Condon uneasy.

Then his mind became occupied with other things. If the cattle were already on the slope, with Gregory's men riding their tails, they would be hard to stampede. The confusion would be so great that any attempt to terrorize them would be useless.

'They got the herd away from us,' Condon said to Moses.

'Aye, that's true,' Moses answered. 'It could be to your advantage.'

'How?'

'We'll stampede this quiet herd that's waiting here. They'll pour over the edge, sweeping the men and cattle that are on the slope down with them.'

Condon saw the advantage of this, but he also realized the deadly implications. Gregory's men were on the slope; the stampede, taking them by surprise from behind, would give them little chance to escape. He thought of Gregory's men—Ace Longest, Colt Denger, Mex Embozo and the others. Then he thought of Arny. Was Arny down there? There was no way to win half a victory; there had to be total success or total failure. The men would have to take their own chances.

'You should have a horse,' Condon said before agreeing to the plan.

'Don't worry about me. Make your decision, boy.'

'All right. You stay here, and I'll circle the herd. When I get ready on the other side, I'll fire my gun and turn the dogs loose.'

'Aye,' Moses agreed cryptically.

It was getting light fast as Condon made his way around the still quiet herd. He estimated there were at least two thousand cattle there; maybe more. Condon could see no herders from where he was, and decided that what herders there were must be at the north side of the herd on the edge of the mesa, holding the cattle back until Gregory signaled for them. In his desperation to get the cattle loaded and out of there, Gregory had spread his men very thin.

Condon reached the other side of the herd without incident. Some of the cattle were still lying down. Suppose they failed to booger? Suppose the dogs and his gunshots only brought disaster? It was too late to think of that now. He got off his horse and loosed the dogs. Then vaulting to the saddle, he fired his gun and yelled at the dogs. Far across the herd, Condon heard an unearthly scream. It was like a soul in torment crying out for mercy. Then the dogs set up their baying, and the cattle rose as one brute entity, congealed into a frightened, bawling mass, and headed toward the edge of the mesa!

The die was cast. Firing his gun, Condon

spurred his horse after the herd, keeping them in one direction, while the dogs added their tumult to the deadly confusion. Reaching the edge of the mesa, the cattle surged over, unable to stop, fighting to keep their footing. The cattle at the front of the stampede smashed into the back of the herd that was on its way to be loaded, and no power on earth could stop them. They were hurled and battered forward by the weight of the cattle in the rear.

Condon started down the trail on the heels of the cattle. Daylight was now like liquid glass, clear but distorting. Condon kept pulling the trigger of his gun after it was empty. He reloaded on the run. He had lost sight of the dogs, who were scattered, howling, into the herd. Far off he could still hear Moses' weird scream, and then the scream stopped. Condon had no time to wonder about it. He heard other men shouting, other guns firing, and, looking below, he could see the river through the cloud of dust. The herd, which was being loaded, catching the hysteria of excitement, stampeded into the barges, into the river. Condon had stopped shooting; the shots were no longer necessary.

Fighting his way ahead along the side of the herd, Condon felt his horse hop, slide and stumble down the rugged water courses. He looked across the sea of bobbing backs and caught his breath. He saw Cal Moses mounted on a steer, hanging to a horn with one hand, and with the other slapping and whipping with his hat. Moses had said he needed neither gun nor horse. He was proving this, but at what price? He could never come through the stampede alive; the odds were against him. If he fell from the bare back of the plunging steer, the sharp hooves would cut him to ribbons.

Condon was getting close to the bottom of the trail, and he could see the drama at the river. There was a confusion of men shouting, cattle bawling. Condon brushed the dust and sweat from his eyes and thought he was dreaming. Some of the shots sounded as if they were coming from the direction of the Hanker ferry. Who could be siding him from Hanker? He had no time to think about this before he saw the figure of Naomi, her hat gone, her dark hair blowing in the wind like a raven's wing. She had not ridden home as he had ordered her. She had gone on ahead, thinking they would stampede the herd being loaded, as planned, instead of the herd that was waiting behind. Now she was caught with the rest of Gregory's crew.

Condon knew that he had to catch up with her, that he had to protect her from the cattle swarming upon her. Forgetting his own danger, he rode into the stampede, praying his horse would keep his footing. Once down, nothing could save him. He was able to worm his way forward. He saw Gregory on one of the barges, beating at the cattle with his good arm as though to hold them back. Then he saw Ace Longest on the river bank, shouting curses at Naomi.

'You blasted wench—you're the one who started all this, you Indian lover! I'll fix you!'

Ace's voice carried to Condon. Condon saw Ace raise his gun and knew he could not reach Naomi in time. He shouted at Ace, but he didn't even know what he was saying. Naomi's horse splashed into the water as Ace fired. At the same instant a man leaped from the nearest barge and threw himself in front of her. The man jerked like a puppet as Ace's bullets smashed into him before he dragged Naomi from her horse and into the water with him.

Condon reached the river, rolled from his horse and waded into the churning water. The cattle had slowed their pell mell stampede at the water's edge, being forced reluctantly into the stream and across it to scatter into the washes and gullies. Condon saw Naomi holding a burden in her arms. He pushed his way through the current toward her, praying under his breath. Not until he got the girl and her burden on shore did he recognize the man who had saved her life. He looked down into the wet, placid face of Mex Embozo.

His first thought was of Naomi. 'Are you all right?' he asked her. There was no time to scold her now.

'I'm all right, thanks to him,' she said, looking at the dying man.

There was a froth of blood on Embozo's lips, a blossom of blood upon his chest. 'My saint has chosen wisely between us, *señorita*.' He smiled. 'She could not save both. To you I leave my horse and saddle. *Madre de Dios*, what a place to die. For once my old mother would be proud of me, *amigos*.' His head dropped, and it was all over for Mex Embozo. Condon silently thanked heaven that he would not have to take such a man back for hanging.

'Are you sure you're all right?' he asked Naomi.

Tears mingled with the water on her face. 'I'm all right.'

'Keep down and keep out of trouble,' he told her. 'I've got to find Ace Longest.'

He rode away, the face of the Mexican still haunting him. How had a man with such instincts for good chosen evil ways? There was no such saving grace in Ace Longest. Condon would gladly cut the rope that would drop Ace to his death, but first he had to catch him. He could see him nowhere on the river bank. He rode cautiously, wondering why none of the other Massacre men had tried to stop him. Then he realized they were

176

busy fighting cattle and other men. He did not know which other men, but supposed some fight had started between Kile's men and the Massacre. Then he saw Ace Longest down-river near the ferry, swimming his horse across the river and heading for Hanker.

Condon forgot everything but that Ace had tried to kill Naomi—that Ace had vowed to kill him. He would give Ace his chance—to surrender or die. But it might not be Ace who died. That was a chance he had to take. There was Colt Denger to reckon with; Colt, who had killed Tex Lowman. Then he thought of Arny, and tried to put him out of his mind. Arny was back there with the owlhoots and long-ropers he had chosen, and there was no way he could be saved unless he saved himself.

Condon swam the big pinto crossways of the current, spurring him in above the ferry so that he would drift down to the ferry landing. Busy with the river and his horse Condon lost sight of Ace. That didn't stop him. He rode Bolo out of the water and up the Hanker trail. He had never been in Hanker, but he knew cow towns, outlaw hangouts and deadfalls. Ace would head for Hanker, hoping to find either asylum or assistance. Vaguely he thought of Gregory, and remembered him making a futile effort to stem the tide of flesh. What happened to

Patch and Maxine? To Emma? Had he brought destruction upon them all? Had he wreaked vengeance on friend and foe alike? Tex was dead; Cal Moses could never survive the stampede. Naomi was alive only through the fatal gesture of a gallant man. Ace Longest was the root of all this evil—and the root must die.

Hanker was no more than he had expected—a shanty town. The biggest building and the gaudiest was the Gay Lady Saloon. He headed toward it and saw people moving furtively out of his way. They knew the showdown had come and wondered who would die. Condon dismounted at the rail, leaving the reins drag. He walked across the board walk and kicked open the bat doors of the saloon. A skeleton of a man sat at a table, his eyes hooded and his bony fingers riffling a deck of cards. Against the bar stood a woman, still in her prime, but with hard lines gathering in her face. There was no sign of Ace Longest or Colt Denger. The rear door of the saloon was still swinging partly ajar, signaling a hasty exit. Nobody said a word; nobody needed to talk, for the death in the air spoke louder than words.

Condon backed out and slid around the side of the building, which faced a vacant lot. He did not look up to see the face staring down at him from the upstairs window. Ace Longest was somewhere in that shack town;

that was all he could think of. Ace Longest was there, and the town would be his Boot Hill. He slid around the corner at the rear of the building and skirted the steps leading up to the porch on the second floor. He came to a shed, kicked the door open and jumped back. The shed was empty.

Ace was in the town somewhere, Condon was certain, and Ace would kill him on sight. Condon darted across the dusty road and made his way to the barn in back of Prentiss' general store. There were cracks wider than a man's thumb between the boards of the wall, and putting an eye to one of them, Condon scanned the interior. There was a pile of hay, but he saw no movement in it, and chancing a shot in the back, he sidled to the door and entered the barn. From there he could watch the street.

He saw Colt Denger ride wildly into town and stop before the Iron Bucket saloon. Moments later he came out with Ace Longest and walked across the dusty road to the Gay Lady. Condon didn't stop to wonder about this. Here was the showdown, and he was relieved it had come. Rising stiffly, his chaps still wet from the swim across the river on Bolo, he stalked out of the barn and directly to the Gay Lady. He saw nothing but the batwing doors ahead of him; he saw nothing down the road or up the road. He hitched his gun around, hoping his shoulder had healed enough not to slow his draw. Then he batted the doors open.

Colt Denger was part way up the stairs when Condon stepped inside. Ace Longest was at the far end of the bar, ordering a drink from the handsome woman Condon had seen before. Denger turned and stopped on the fourth step, one hand gripping the railing, and the soggy quirly dropped from his thin lips. Ace backed away from the bar, his hands stiff at his thighs.

'I'm taking you, Ace, for murder and cattle rustling on the Delgado range in Colorado,' Condon said distinctly.

'You ain't got jurisdiction here, hombre,' Ace said quietly.

'I've got all the jurisdiction I need, Ace. You tried to kill me twice; maybe three times will be a charm.'

'Don't think it won't. I've waited for this, mister. It will give me something satisfying to think of when I leave here.'

Denger shouted, 'Cut it out, Ace. We came here to see the boss; we didn't come here for a killing!'

'Maybe you didn't.'

'Drop your gun, Ace,' Condon ordered.

Ace made his move, flicking like the head of a rattler. Condon had one sharp moment of misgiving as he snatched for his gun. One unhealed fiber in his arm, one fiber out of a million, could slow his bullet one breath. He

180

threw himself sideways and felt Ace's bullet smash across his ribs. Then he had his own gun free. Denger was to one side and back of him, and to Denger a back was fair game. Ace had to go. Condon's gun jumped in his hand, and he heard the bullet as it hit Ace's guts with a squashy sound. Ace fired again, but the shot went downward into the floor as Ace sank to his knees. Ace was through, but he could live the extra seconds to get off another shot. Condon needed those seconds for Colt Denger. He heard a commotion behind him and shots and braced himself for a slug in the back, but there was none. He turned to see Denger diving over the railing like a rag man. Then he heard Ace's last shot, and his feet were knocked out from under him and he fell in a heap on the floor.

Condon sat up, staring at the heel that had been shot off his boot, and let him fall. He looked at Ace Longest, but Ace was through forever. Still wondering why Denger hadn't shot him, Condon rose slowly on his uneven boots and became aware of the people who had crowded into the Gay Lady. He heard his brother Arny's voice close beside him.

'That rattler was aiming to back-shoot you, Cliff. It's a good thing we got here in time.' Arny was holstering a smoking gun.

'What are you doing here, Arny?'

'Same as you, I guess—cleaning up this Massacre mess. I heard there was a stranger

181

loose on the mesa, but I didn't dream it was you. I helped with the rustling at Delgado because I thought you were top-dogging me. But when they killed Hal Chester it made me see how wrong I was. I played along with them, hoping to get even for Hal's murder. I sent a wire from Tooker days ago; and I stopped the stage between Tooker and Hanker trying to get the letter telling when Kile would be there. These men with me are reps I wired for from the other ranges that were robbed.'

'Yep,' a raw-boned man spoke up, 'we got here just after the barges. We were wondering how we could fight the Kile men and also the Massacre men. Then came that stampede down the hill. That simplified matters like all get-out. We got some of the hombres tied up on one of the barges. The others are dead or scattered. The cattle are spread out in the cut-banks, but we can dig them out and examine the brands with the magnifying glasses which we brung.'

Condon had his arm on Arny's shoulder and tried to ignore the burning cut across his ribs. 'I thought you were Satan's child for sure, Arny. Forgive me.'

'I could have been, Cliff. I guess I growed up.'

Then Condon was surprised to see Naomi standing on the stairs so she could see over the crowd. He hobbled over to her on his crooked boots.

'Thank God you're all right, honey,' he said, and he kissed her before all of them.

When he released her, he heard a sound at the top of the stairs and, looking up, saw Emma standing there, wearing a becoming dress. She was no char-woman meekly taking orders; she was a figure of strength, authority and determination.

'Come on up here, you two,' she said to Condon and Naomi.

With his arm about Naomi, Condon hobbled up the stairs and into Vinnie Goode's sitting room. The place was tastefully and comfortably furnished.

'Set,' Emma said. 'This might take a while.'

Condon and Naomi sat on a sofa, and Emma took a chair facing them.

'You hurt, son?' she asked.

'A scratch on my ribs, and my boot heel's shot off.'

'You were lucky. When Max brought you in and I drained you of gangrene, I never thought you were going to be an avenging angel. I guess it's better this way.'

'Where's Maxine?' Naomi asked, concerned.

'When she got home yesterday, she acted a mite strange, like a person running from a haunt. She insisted on leaving the Massacre at once with that feller Clay Jordan; allowed she

183

was going to marry him in Denver. She wanted to get away before Vern Gregory knew about it.'

'You mean she was running away from her own father?' Condon asked.

'He wasn't her father,' Emma said patiently. 'It's time for confession. I'll try to make it clear how the Massacre started. Charley Beyer, my husband, made a fairly good strike near Denver and allowed he was going to build himself a cattle empire. He was a blond giant of a man. He insisted he was going to make me a queen, reigning over a whole territory. He left me in Denver with two babies to collect the money for the claim, while he went on ahead with a company of immigrants to find his ranch. Then he was coming for us. The time kept stretching out, but he didn't come. It was a hard winter.

'I got acquainted with Vern Gregory, a hothead from Virginia who had a grudge to settle against the Yankees. He thought he was a gambler, but he didn't know enough not to draw to an inside straight. After I collected the money for the claim, I staked Vern Gregory for a time, but he kept losing. He owed me, but he couldn't pay, so he offered to help me get back East. I didn't want to go back East; I wanted Charley. So he agreed to go with me to look for him. In early spring I bought an outfit, and we started trailing after Charley—me with two babies, and Gregory with Patch, the Negro slave boy who followed him like a dog.

'We moved on from camp to settlement, to trading post until we reached Hanker. There I heard rumors about the massacre. I met Vinnie and her mother at the time, and I left the babies with them. I left Gregory with his cards. I took a pack and headed across the mesa. It was beautiful, virgin country, alive with game and with forests of trees near the high mountain. I was puzzled that Charley would look any farther for a ranch, but he'd always talked of California.

'My second day out, I came across tracks that the winter had almost blotted out, and they wandered across the mesa as though lost. The third day I came to the scene of the massacre: pieces of wagons, the charred remains of fires. I saw rude crosses made out of scraps marking graves. I felt the cold chill of death still in that camp as I tried to riddle out what had happened. Then I saw him, squatting in the junipers some distance away. He was a white man with wild hair and beard, and he was watching me with stony eyes like a wild animal. Somehow I knew the truth. He was Charley, my husband. He was no longer a blond giant, but a bent, furtive thing, and it sickened me to look at him.

'I walked toward him, calling his name. He didn't recognize me. He kept shaking his head, muttering, "No more left—no more

185

left." I went to him, and he didn't try to run away. I knelt beside him and put my arms around him. I called him by name, and soon I saw a flash of recognition in his eyes, but it quickly died. He babbled out a strange, weird story. They had been told there was a trail down the south side of the mesa that would save them two hundred miles on their way to California. They couldn't find the trail but got lost in the high country. A raid band of Indians found them, took their horses and supplies and left them there without guns or ammunition. The winter came on suddenly, and they starved, and the ones who lived ate the ones who died. Charley was the only one to survive until spring, when he began eating roots and berries and anything he could find except flesh.

'He wouldn't leave there. I don't know whether he knew me or not. He said he had to stay there and make atonement. His mind had been twisted by the horrible experience. That's when I made my plan. I made a deal with Gregory that he could be the king of the Massacre if he would raise Maxine as his own child. She was a beautiful, golden-haired child.'

'There's no use going into details. We built the ranch, stocked it, and I was content to live in the log cabin and be near Maxine and watch her grow into a queen. I kept Naomi with me.'

'You mean Cal Moses is my father?' Naomi gasped.

'And Maxine's father.' Emma nodded. 'She is your sister.'

'Does she know about this?'

'Does she have to know,' Emma asked.

Condon said, unbelieving, 'Cal Moses has lived out there all these years trying to find forgiveness? He was always writing in a book . . .'

'He writes what happened over and over, hoping it will shrivel his soul. Maybe I can help him find peace now,' Emma said. 'I knew Naomi was for you the first time I saw you, Condon. You two can have the Massacre. A lot of those cattle belonged to the Massacre.'

'I could send Arny back for my mother,' Condon said.

There was a knock on the door, and at Emma's word it opened to reveal Patch standing there.

'What is it, Patch?' Emma asked.

'That theah old Cal Moses, he done took the dogs and went back to his shack. Mistah Gregory, he was killed by the cattle. I dragged him out of the watah. Could Ah bury him on the Massacre, ma'am, befoah I go away?'

'Of course we'll bury him on the Massacre, Patch. Where do you think you're going?'

'Ah was his man, ma'am. Ah kept his

secrets, knowing some of them was bad.'

'You're going to stay here with us, Patch,' Condon said. 'We need you.'

'There are no more secrets, Patch,' Naomi chimed in.

'And there aren't going to be,' Condon said, drawing Naomi close and kissing her. 'We've got a lot of work to do, so we'd better get at it.'

Photoset, printed and bound in Great Britain by REDWOOD BURN LIMITED, Trowbridge, Wiltshire